Kate Hewitt

THE ITALIAN'S BOUGHT BRIDE

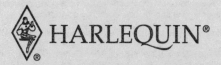

HARLEQUIN®

TORONTO • NEW YORK • LONDON
AMSTERDAM • PARIS • SYDNEY • HAMBURG
STOCKHOLM • ATHENS • TOKYO • MILAN • MADRID
PRAGUE • WARSAW • BUDAPEST • AUCKLAND

Recycling programs
for this product may
not exist in your area.

ISBN-13: 978-0-373-12800-6
ISBN-10:   0-373-12800-2

THE ITALIAN'S BOUGHT BRIDE

First North American Publication 2009.

Copyright © 2008 by Kate Hewitt.

All about the author…
Kate Hewitt

KATE HEWITT discovered her first Harlequin romance novel while on a trip to England when she was thirteen, and she's continued to read them ever since. She wrote her first story at the age of five, simply because her older brother had written one and she thought she could do it, too. That story was one sentence long—fortunately, they've become a bit more detailed as she's grown older.

She studied drama in college and, shortly after graduation, moved to New York City to pursue a career in theater. This was derailed by something far better—meeting the man of her dreams, who happened also to be her older brother's childhood friend. Ten days after their wedding, they moved to England, where Kate worked a variety of different jobs—drama teacher, editorial assistant, youth worker, secretary and, finally, mother.

When her oldest daughter was a year old, Kate sold her first short story to a British magazine. Since then she has sold many stories and serials, but writing romance novels remains her first love, of course!

Besides writing, she enjoys reading, traveling and learning to knit—it's an ongoing process and she's made a lot of scarves. After having lived in England for six years, she now resides in Connecticut with her husband, her three young children and, possibly one day, a dog.

Kate loves to hear from readers. You can contact her through her Web site, www.kate-hewitt.com.

To Abby, for being a wonderful friend and confidant.
You've seen my tears! Love K.

CHAPTER ONE

STEFANO CAPOZZI SAT in the well-appointed office of one of Milan's top psychiatrists, his eyes glittering in a face set like stone.

'It has been eight months,' he said flatly, even though Renaldo Speri had the case notes on his desk. 'Eight months of every treatment available, imaginable, and no change.'

Speri smiled in sympathetic understanding. 'You cannot expect a miracle cure, Signor Capozzi. You may not be able to expect a cure at all.' He trailed off as he took in Stefano's unrelenting gaze.

Stefano shook his head. 'I want better.'

He would have better. He wouldn't accept brush-offs or excuses. He'd come to Milan to find the best therapist for the child in his charge, and he would have it.

Speri ran a hand through his thinning hair and sighed. 'Signor Capozzi, you must face the very real possibility that Lucio falls on the spectrum of pervasive development disorder—'

'No.' After eight months of Lucio's silence and stress, he would not accept it. He was used to obstacles in business, and personal ones would prove no different, no more difficult. 'Lucio was normal before his father died. He was like any other child—'

'Autism often manifests itself at three years of age,' Speri explained gently. 'Lucio had only a little speech before his father's death, and lost it completely in the months afterwards.'

Stefano raised one eyebrow in scathing scepticism. 'And you are now trying to tell me that the two aren't related?'

'I am trying to tell you that it is a possibility,' Speri said, his voice becoming strained with patience. 'As difficult as it may be to accept.'

Stefano was silent for a moment. 'There is no cure for autism,' he finally said. He'd done his research. He'd read the books, seen the statistics.

'There are therapies, diets, that alleviate some of the symptoms,' Speri said quietly. 'And it also depends where he falls on the spectrum—'

'He's not on the spectrum.'

'Signor—'

'I want something else.' Stefano levelled his gaze at the psychiatrist and waited.

After a moment Speri raised his hands in a defeated gesture. 'Signor Capozzi, we have tried therapies and grief counselling, and as you've reminded me, there has been no change. If anything, Lucio has descended deeper into his own iron-walled world. If this were a case of normal grief—'

'What,' Stefano asked icily, 'is normal about grief?'

'The grieving process is normal,' Speri said steadily. 'And accepted. But Lucio's behaviour is not normal, and there should have been signs of improvement in communication by now. There have been none.'

On his lap, out of sight, Stefano's hand curled into a fist. 'I know that.'

'Then accept that he might fall on the spectrum, and turn to the therapies and treatments that can help him best!'

Stefano was silent. Carefully, deliberately, he flattened his hand, resting it on the desktop. When Lucio's mother, Bianca, had asked him to help, to come to Milan and tell 'those doctors' that her son was not autistic, Stefano had accepted. He had believed Bianca then, but now he felt the first flicker of doubt.

He would do anything for Bianca, anything for Lucio. Their

family had saved him all those years ago, had pulled him up from the mire of his upbringing, giving him the steps and tools to be the man he was today.

He would never forget it.

'Surely there is something we haven't tried,' he said at last. 'Before we accept this diagnosis.'

'The psychiatrists involved in an autism diagnosis are very thorough,' Speri said. 'And competent. They do not make such a judgement incautiously.'

'Agreed,' Stefano said tersely. 'But still—is there something else?'

Speri was silent for a long moment. 'There is,' he finally said, his voice reluctant, 'a therapist who had success with a child who'd been diagnosed with autism. Misdiagnosed, as the case turned out. He'd suffered a severe trauma the therapists working with him were unaware of, and when it was uncovered he began to regain his speech.'

Hope—treacherous, desperate—unfurled within him. 'Then couldn't Lucio be like that boy?' Stefano demanded.

'I don't want to offer you false hope,' Speri said, and the reluctance in his voice became more pronounced. 'That was one case—an anomaly, a fluke—'

Stefano cut him off; he didn't want to hear about anomalies. He wanted hope, he wanted certainty. 'Who is this therapist?'

'She's an art therapist,' Speri said. 'Often creative therapies help children release suppressed emotions and memories, as was the case with this child. However, Lucio's symptoms are more severe...'

'Creative therapies,' Stefano repeated. He didn't like the sound of it. It sounded abstract, absurd. 'What exactly do you mean?'

'She uses the creative arts to provide an outlet, whether through art, song or performance, for a child's suppressed emotions. Sometimes it is the key that can unlock a child who has been unable to be reached.'

Unlock. It was an apt word, Stefano thought, when he considered Lucio's blank face and staring eyes. And no words. Not one word spoken in nearly a year.

'All right, then,' he said shortly. 'We'll try it. I want her.'

'It was one case—' Speri began, and Stefano silenced him with a raised hand.

'I want her.'

'She lives in London. I read of the case in a journal and we corresponded briefly, but I don't know…'

'She's English?' Disappointment sliced through him. Of what use to him—to Lucio—was an English therapist?

'No, I wouldn't have mentioned her if that was the case,' Speri said with a faint smile. 'She's Italian, but I don't believe she's been back to Italy in many years.'

'She'll come,' Stefano said firmly. He would make sure of it—offer whatever enticements or inducements she needed. 'How long did she work with this other child?'

'A few months—'

'Then I want her in Abruzzo, with Lucio, as soon as possible.' Stefano spoke with a finality that took the psychiatrist aback.

'Signor Capozzi, she'll have other patients, responsibilities—'

'She can get rid of them.'

'It's not that simple.'

'Yes,' Stefano said flatly. 'It is. It will be. Lucio can't be moved; it's too upsetting for him. She'll come to Abruzzo. And stay.'

Speri shifted uncomfortably. 'That will be for you to negotiate with her, of course. Such an intensive course is to be recommended, although there are no guarantees, but it is also costly…'

'Money,' Stefano replied with the barest flicker of a smile, 'is no object.'

'Naturally.' Speri looked down at his notes; Stefano knew the highlights of his own CV were sketched there. Stefano Capozzi, founder of Capozzi Electronica. Liquidator of a dozen of Italy's top electronics firms. Unrivalled.

'I'll give you her details,' Speri said with a little sigh of ca-pitulation. 'I have the article about her and the case I mentioned here. I should tell you she's young, quite newly qualified, rela-tively inexperienced, but of course that case was remarkable…'

'That boy recovered? He spoke again?' Stefano demanded. He didn't like the flicker of compassion—or was it pity?—in the doctor's eyes.

'Yes,' Speri said quietly, 'he did. But it isn't that simple, Signor Capozzi. And Lucio might be different. He might indeed be—'

'Her details, please.' Stefano held out his hand. He didn't expect things to be simple. He just wanted them *started*.

'Just a moment…' Speri looked through his papers again. 'Ah, here's the article I mentioned.' He smiled and handed Stefano a medical journal, opened to a folded page. 'Here she is…a lovely photograph, don't you think? Allegra Avesti is her name.'

Stefano didn't hear the last part of what Speri had said, but then he didn't need to. He knew her name. He knew her.

Or at least, he once had.

Allegra Avesti. The woman who should have been his wife, the woman he no longer knew.

His concern for Lucio fell away for a moment as he gazed at the caption: 'Allegra Avesti, Art Therapist, with patient'. Memories swam to the surface and he forced them back down again, drowning them as his dispassionate gaze moved to the photo. He saw that she was older, thinner. She was smiling in the photo, hazel eyes glinting as she looked at the child by her side, his little fists pounding a lump of clay.

Her head was tilted to one side, her hair, a thousand shades of sunlight, piled in a careless knot, tendrils escaping to trail her cheek, her shoulder.

Her eyes sparkled and her smile was wide, encouraging, full of hope. He could almost hear the tinkling promise of pure joy. She had dimples, he saw. He'd never known. He'd never seen them. Had she not laughed like that in his presence?

Perhaps not.

He stared at the picture—the ghost of a girl he'd once known, an image of a woman he'd never met.

Allegra.

His Allegra…except she wasn't, he knew that, had known it when he'd waited while she'd walked away. For ever.

He closed the journal, handed it back to Speri. Thought of Lucio. Only Lucio. 'Indeed, a lovely picture,' he said without any intonation or expression. The look of joy and hope on Allegra's face would be an inspiration to many a fearful and weary parent, seeking answers for their child. 'I shall contact her.'

Speri nodded. 'And if for some reason she is occupied, we can discuss…alternatives…'

Stefano acknowledged this statement with a brusque nod. He knew Allegra would not be busy. He would make sure she was not. If she was the best, if she'd helped a child like Lucio, he would have her.

Even if it was Allegra.

Especially if it was Allegra.

The past, he vowed, would not matter when it came to helping Lucio. The past would not matter at all.

Allegra Avesti gazed into the mirror of the ladies' powder room at the Dorchester Hotel and grimaced. Her hair was meant to be in a carelessly elegant chignon, but it looked as if she'd only succeeded with the first part of that plan.

At least her dress hit the right note, she decided with satisfaction. Smoky-grey silk, cut severely across the collarbone and held up by two skinny straps on each shoulder, it was elegant and sexy without being too revealing.

It had cost a fortune, far more than she could afford on her earnings as a therapist. Yet she'd wanted to look good for her cousin Daphne's wedding. She'd wanted to feel good.

As if she fitted in.

Except, she knew, she didn't. Not really. Not since the night she'd fled her own wedding and left everyone else to pick up the scattered pieces.

With a little sigh she took a lipstick and blusher out of her handbag. She didn't think of that night, chose never to think of it—the shattered dream, the broken heart. The betrayal, the fear.

Yet her cousin's wedding this evening had brought her own almost-wedding to the forefront of her mind, and it had taken all her energy and emotion to push it back into the box where she liked to keep those memories. That life.

The wedding had been lovely, a candlelit ceremony at a small London church. Daphne, with her heart-shaped face, soft voice and cloud of dark hair, had looked tremulously beautiful. Her husband, a high-flyer at an advertising firm in the City, seemed a bit too self-assured for Allegra's taste, but she hoped her cousin had found happiness. Love. If such things could truly be found.

Yet, during the ceremony, she'd listened to the vows they'd spoken with undisguised cynicism.

'Will you love her, comfort her, honour and protect her, and, forsaking all others, be faithful to her as long as you both shall live?'

As the words had washed over her, Allegra couldn't help but think of her own wedding day, the day that never happened, the vows she'd never spoken.

Stefano hadn't loved her, wouldn't comfort her or honour her. Protect her? Yes, she thought wryly, he would have done that. Faithful? Doubtful…

Yet she still felt, sitting in that dimly lit church, an unidentifiable stab of longing, of something almost like regret.

Except she didn't regret anything. She certainly didn't regret walking out on Stefano. Although her uncle—and sometimes it seemed the rest of society—blamed her for that fiasco, Allegra knew the real fiasco would have been if she'd stayed.

But she was free, she told herself firmly. She was free and happy.

Allegra turned away from the mirror. She'd survived Daphne's wedding, slipping out before anyone could corner her, but she wasn't looking forward to the reception tonight. She was in a melancholy mood, didn't feel like chatting and laughing and dancing. And although she loved Daphne and her Aunt Barbara, her relationship with her Uncle George had always been strained.

She hadn't spoken to her uncle more than a handful of times in the seven years since he'd first sheltered her when she'd fled Italy, and those conversations had been uncomfortable at best.

Straightening, she left the luxurious powder room. It had been a hell of a day—running from appointment to appointment at the hospital, grappling with one serious and seemingly hopeless case after another. There had been no breakthroughs, no breath of hope.

Not today.

She loved her job, loved it with an intensity that some said should be replaced with the love of—and for—a man, but Allegra knew she was happy as she was. Happy and free, she reminded herself again firmly.

Still, the hopelessness of some of her cases, the children who had seen far too much suffering, too much sorrow, wore her down. She only had a few moments with them, perhaps an hour a week at most, and doctors expected breakthroughs. Parents expected miracles.

Once in a while, God was good. Once in a while they happened.

But not today.

The reception was being held in the Orchid Room, with its walls of delicate blue and ornate painted scrollery. A string quartet had been arranged near a parquet dance floor, and guests circulated amidst waiters bearing trays of hors d'oeuvres and sparkling champagne.

Allegra surveyed the glittering crowd and lifted her chin. She wasn't used to this. She didn't go to parties.

The last party she'd attended—a party like this, with society in full swing—had been for her own engagement. She'd worn a poufy, pink dress and heels that had pinched her feet, and she'd been so happy. So excited.

She shook her head as if to banish the thought, the memory. Why was she thinking—remembering—those days now? Why was she letting the memories sift through her mind like ghosts from another life—a life that had never happened? A life she'd run away from.

It was the wedding tonight, she decided. It was the first one she'd attended since she'd abandoned her own.

Forget it, Allegra told herself as she plucked a flute of champagne from one of the circulating trays and made her way through the crowd. Her cousin's wedding was bound to stir up some unpleasant memories, unpalatable feelings. That was all this mood was, and she could deal with it.

Allegra took a sip of champagne, let the bubbles fizz defiantly through her and surveyed the milling crowd.

'Allegra…I'm so glad you could come.'

She turned to see her Aunt Barbara smiling uncertainly at her. Dowdy but cheerful, Barbara Mason wore a lime coloured evening gown that did nothing for her pasty complexion or grey-streaked hair.

Allegra smiled warmly back. 'I'm glad to be here as well,' she returned a little less than truthfully. 'I'm so thrilled for Daphne.'

'Yes…they'll be very happy, don't you think?' Barbara's anxious gaze flitted to her daughter, who was chatting and smiling, her husband's arm around her shoulders.

'I'm afraid I don't know much about the groom,' Allegra said, taking another sip of champagne. 'His name is Charles?'

'Charles Edmunds. They met at work. You know Daphne's been a PA at Hobbs and Ford?'

Allegra nodded. Although her uncle disapproved of Allegra keeping in touch with his family, she still spoke to Barbara on the telephone every few months, and several times Daphne had defied her father to meet Allegra for lunch.

She'd learned at one of those outings that Daphne had secured a job as PA at an advertising firm, despite her obvious lack of qualifications. Her father's, apparently, had been enough.

'I'm happy for them,' she said. She watched Charles Edmunds as he glanced down at his wife, smiling easily. Then he raised his eyes, surveying the ballroom with a gaze that was steely and grey. Looking for business contacts, associates? Allegra wondered cynically. Someone worth knowing, at any rate, she decided as his eyes passed over her and Barbara without a flicker.

So much for true love, she thought with a little grimace. Charles Edmunds was a man like most others—cold, ambitious, on the prowl.

'Barbara!' Her uncle's sharp voice cut across the murmur of the crowd. Both Allegra and her aunt tensed as George Mason strode towards them, his narrow features sharpened by dislike as he glanced at his niece.

'Barbara, you should see to your guests,' he commanded tersely, and Barbara offered Allegra a quick, defeated smile of apology. Allegra smiled back.

'It was good to see you, Allegra,' Barbara murmured. 'We don't see enough of you,' she added with a shred of defiance. George motioned her away with a shooing gesture, and Barbara went.

There was a moment of tense silence and Allegra swivelled the slick, moisture-beaded stem of her champagne flute between her fingers, wondering what to say to a man who had ordered her from his house seven years ago. The few times she'd seen him since, at increasingly infrequent family gatherings, they'd avoided each other.

Now they were face to face.

He looked the same as ever, she saw as she slid him a glance from beneath her lashes. Thin, grey-haired, well-dressed, precise. Cold eyes and a prim, pursed mouth. Absolutely no humour.

'Thank you for inviting me, Uncle George,' Allegra finally said. 'It was good of you, considering.'

'I had to invite you, Allegra,' George replied. 'You're family, even though you've hardly acted like it in the last seven years.'

Allegra pressed her lips together to keep from uttering a sharp retort. She wasn't the one who had ordered so-called family out of his house, and who had made it increasingly difficult for Allegra to stay in touch.

Running away had been her only crime, and her uncle never failed to remind her of it.

For in running away she'd shamed him. Allegra still remembered her uncle's fury when she'd shown up, terrified and exhausted, on his doorstep.

'You can stay the night,' he'd said grimly, 'and then you need to be gone.'

'He does business with Stefano Capozzi,' her aunt had explained, desperate for Allegra to understand and not to judge. 'If he's seen sheltering you, Capozzi could make life very unpleasant for him, Allegra. For all of us.'

It had been an *unpleasant* insight into her former fiancé's character. She had wondered then if Stefano would come for her, find her. Make life unpleasant for *her*.

He hadn't, and as far as she knew he'd never made life unpleasant for her uncle. She wondered sometimes whether that had been a convenient excuse for George Mason to wash his hands of her, especially when her own defection had been followed so quickly by her mother's.

Her mother…another person, another life, Allegra chose not to remember.

Now she met her uncle's cold gaze. 'I needed help and you gave it to me,' she said levelly. Her fingers tightened on the stem of her glass. 'I'll always be grateful for that.'

'And you'll show it by keeping out of my way,' George finished coolly. 'And Daphne's. Her nerves are strung high enough as it is.'

Allegra felt a flush creeping up her throat, staining her face. She kept her chin high. 'I certainly don't want to cause any dismay to my cousin. I'll pay my respects and leave as soon as possible.'

'Good,' he replied shortly before moving off.

Allegra straightened proudly. She felt as if every eye in the faceless crowd was focused on her, seeing, knowing, condemning, even though she knew no one cared.

Except her uncle and his family.

A waiter passed and Allegra placed her nearly untouched champagne on his tray.

Murmuring her excuses as she moved through the crowd, she found a secluded corner of the ballroom and took her position there, half hidden behind a potted palm.

She took a deep breath and surveyed the circulating crowd. No one was paying any attention to her, she knew, because she wasn't important. Her flight from Italy seven years ago was little cause of concern or even gossip these days.

She'd kept her head down and well out of society's glare these last years, working two jobs to pay for her schooling. She was far, far from this glamorous crowd, the glittering lifestyle. Yet the people who knew her, who were supposed to love her…what had happened seven years ago still mattered to them. And it always would.

It didn't bother her on a day-to-day basis. She didn't need these people. She had a new life now, a good one. When she'd left that night, she'd gained her freedom, but the price for that freedom had been, quite literally, everything.

It had been a price worth paying.

The music died down and Allegra saw everyone heading to the tables. Dinner was about to be served.

Taking another deep breath, she moved through the crowds again and found her place card. She was at a table tucked in the back with a motley handful of guests who looked to be nearly as out of place as she was. Distant, vaguely embarrassing relatives, colleagues and friends who necessitated an invitation yet were not an asset to the sparkling and successful party George Mason intended for his daughter.

An art therapist with a disreputable past certainly fitted into that category, Allegra thought ruefully.

With a murmured hello, she took her place between an overweight aunt and a weedy looking businessman. The meal passed in stilted conversations and awkward silences as eight misfits attempted to get along.

Allegra let the conversation wash over her in a meaningless tide of sound and wondered just how soon she could leave.

She wanted to see Daphne but, with the cold, ambitious Charles Edmunds at her cousin's side, Allegra wasn't expecting a cosy cousinly chat.

The plates were cleared and her uncle stood up to speak. Allegra watched him posture importantly, talking about how he knew Charles Edmunds, cracking business jokes. At one point he pontificated on the importance of family and she smothered the stab of resentment that threatened to pierce her composure.

Soon after, the music started up again and Allegra excused herself from the table before anyone could ask her to dance. The junior from Charles's office had been eyeing her with a determined expression.

She moved through the crowds, her head held high, her eyes meeting no one else's.

Daphne stood apart with her husband, pale and luminous in a designer wedding gown that hugged her slight figure before flaring out in a row of ruffles.

'Hello, Daphne,' Allegra said.

Her cousin—the cousin she'd shared summers in Italy with, swimming and laughing and plaiting each other's hair—now turned to her with a worried expression.

'Hh… Hello, Allegra,' she said after a moment, her apprehensive gaze flicking to her husband. 'Have you met Charles?'

Charles Edmunds smiled coolly. 'Yes, your cousin came to our engagement party. Don't you remember, darling?'

He made it sound as if she'd crashed the party. She supposed that was what her attendance felt like. Still, she'd wanted to come, had wanted to show that no matter what they did or thought, she was still family.

'Daphne, I only wanted to congratulate you,' Allegra said quietly. 'I'm afraid I'm going to have to leave a bit early—'

'Oh, Allegra—' Daphne looked both relieved and regretful '—I'm sorry…'

'No, it's fine.' Allegra smiled and squeezed her cousin's hand. 'It's fine. I'm tired anyway. It's been a long day.'

'Thank you,' Daphne whispered, and Allegra wondered just what her cousin was thanking her for. For coming? Or for leaving? Or for simply not making a scene?

As if she ever would. She'd only made one scene in her life, and she didn't plan on doing so again.

'Goodbye,' she murmured, and quickly kissed her cousin's cold cheek.

In the foyer, she found the cloakroom and handed the attendant her ticket. She watched as the woman riffled through the rack of luxury wraps for her own plain and inexpensive coat.

'Here you are, miss.'

'Thank you.'

She was just about to pull it on when she heard a voice—a voice of cool confidence and warm admiration. A voice that slid across her senses and into her soul, stirring up those emotions and memories she'd tried so hard to lock away.

It all came rushing back with that voice—the memories, the fear, the regrets, the betrayal. It hurtled back, making her relive the worst night of her life once more, simply by hearing two little words that she knew, somehow, would change her world for ever.

'Hello, Allegra,' Stefano said.

CHAPTER TWO

Seven years earlier

TOMORROW WOULD BE her wedding day. A day of lacy dresses and sunlit kisses, of magic, of promise, of joy and wonder.

Allegra pressed one hand to her wildly beating heart. Outside the Tuscan villa, night settled softly, stealing over purple-cloaked hills and winding its way through the dusty olive groves.

Inside the warm glow of a lamp cast the room into pools of light and shadow. Allegra surveyed her childhood bedroom: the pink pillows and teddy bears vying for space on her narrow girl's bed, the shelf of well-thumbed Enid Blyton books borrowed from English cousins, her early sketches lovingly framed by her childhood nurse, and lastly—wonderfully—her wedding dress, as frothy a confection as any young bride could wish for, swathed in plastic and hanging from her cupboard door.

She let out a little laugh, a giggle of girlish joy. She was getting married!

She'd met Stefano Capozzi thirteen months ago, at her eighteenth birthday party. She'd seen him as she'd picked her way down the stairs in her new, awkward heels. He'd been waiting at the bottom like Rhett Butler, amber eyes glinting with promise, one hand stretched out to her.

She'd taken his hand as naturally as if she'd known him, as

if she'd expected him to be there. When he'd asked her to dance, she'd simply walked into his arms.

It had been so easy. So right.

And, Allegra thought happily, there hadn't been a misstep since. Stefano had asked her out a handful of times, to restaurants and the theatre and a few local parties. He'd written her letters from Paris and Rome, when he was on business, and sent her flowers and trinkets.

And then he'd asked her to marry him…to be his wife. And he would be her husband.

Another giggle escaped her and she heard an answering echo of a laugh from outside, low, throaty, seductive. Allegra opened the shutter and peeped out; she saw a couple in the shadow of a tree, arms, bodies entwined. The woman's head was thrown back and the man was kissing her neck.

Allegra shivered. Stefano had never kissed her neck. The few times he'd kissed her, he had been chaste, almost brotherly, yet the brush of his lips against her skin had sent a strange sensation pooling deep inside, flooding through her with an unfamiliar, new warmth.

Now she watched, fascinated, as the unknown couple's bodies moved and writhed in a sensuous dance.

She drew in a little breath, her eyes still fastened on the couple, the balmy night air cooling her flushed face. Suddenly she wanted to see Stefano. She wanted to say…what?

That she loved him? She'd never said those three little words, and neither had he, but it hardly mattered. Surely he saw it shining from her eyes every time she looked at him. And, as for Stefano…how could she doubt? He'd sought her out, he'd courted her like a troubadour. Of course he loved her.

Yet now she wanted to see him, talk to him. Touch him.

A blush rose to her face and she turned away from the window and the couple, who had moved further into the shadows, her hands pressed to her hot cheeks.

She'd only seen Stefano with his shirt off once, when they'd all gone swimming in the lake. She'd had a glimpse of bare, brown muscle before she'd jerked her gaze away.

And yet tomorrow they would be married. They would be lovers. She knew as much; even she, kept away in convent school, knew the basics of life. Of sex.

Her mind darted away from the implications, the impossibilities. What vague images her fevered brain conjured were blurred, strange, embarrassing.

Yet she still wanted to see him. Now.

Stefano was a night owl; he'd told her before. Allegra didn't think he'd be in bed yet. He'd be downstairs, in her father's study or library, reading one of his fusty old books.

She could find him.

Taking a breath, Allegra opened her bedroom door and crept down the passage. The soft September air was cool, although perhaps she was just hot.

Her hand was slick on the wrought iron railing as she went down the stairs. In the hall, she heard voices from the library.

'This time tomorrow you will have your little bride,' her father, Roberto, said. He sounded as sleekly satisfied as a tomcat.

'And you will have what you want,' Stefano replied, and Allegra jerked involuntarily at the sound of his voice—cool, urbane, indifferent.

She'd never heard him speak in such a tone before.

'Yes, indeed I will. This is a good business arrangement for us both, Stefano…my son.'

'Indeed it is,' Stefano agreed in a bland tone that still somehow made Allegra shiver. 'I'm pleased that you approached me.'

'And not too bad a price, eh?' Roberto chuckled, an ugly, indulgent sound. Allegra's flesh crawled at the sound—a sound she realized she'd never heard, a sound she'd been protected from. Her father's own callousness. Towards her.

'Allegra's mother has raised her well,' Roberto continued. 'She'll give you five or six *bambinos* and then you can keep her in the country.' He chuckled again. 'She'll know her place. And *I* know a woman in Milan…she's very good.'

'Is she?'

Allegra choked, one fist pressed to her lips. What was her father saying? What was *Stefano* saying?

Their words beat a remorseless echo in her numb brain. *Business arrangement.* A deal to be brokered. A bargain to be had.

A woman to be sold.

They were talking about a marriage. Hers.

She shook her head in mute, instinctive denial.

'Yes,' Roberto said, 'she is. There are many pleasures for the married man, Stefano.'

Stefano gave a light answering laugh. 'That I believe.'

Allegra closed her eyes, her hand still against her mouth. She felt dizzy and strange, her heart thudding hopelessly in her chest.

She took a calming breath and tried to think. To trust. Surely there was some explanation why Stefano was saying the things he was, sounding the way he was. If she just *asked*…it would be all right. Everything would be just as it had been.

'Allegra! What are you doing here?'

Her eyes flew open. Stefano stood in front of her, an expression of concern—or was it annoyance?—on his face. Suddenly Allegra couldn't tell. She wondered if she'd *ever* been able to tell.

Even now, her gaze roved hungrily over his features—the bronzed planes of his cheekbones, the thick chocolate-coloured hair swept away from his forehead, his amber eyes glinting in the dim light.

'I…' Her mouth was dry and the questions died in her heart. 'I couldn't sleep.'

'Too excited, *fiorina?*' Stefano smiled, but now everything had been cast into doubt and Allegra wondered if she saw arrogant amusement in that gesture rather than the tenderness she'd always supposed. 'In less than twelve hours we will be man and wife. Can you not wait until then to see me?' He cupped her cheek, letting his thumb drift to caress her lips. Her mouth parted involuntarily and his smile deepened. 'Go to bed, Allegra. Dream of me.'

He dropped his hand and turned away, dismissing her. Allegra watched him, watched the clean, broad lines of his back, tapering to narrow hips, watched him move away from her.

'Do you love me?' As soon as she'd asked the question, she wished she could bite back the words. Gobble them up and swallow them whole. They sounded desperate, pleading, pathetic.

And yet it was a reasonable question, wasn't it? They were about to be *married*. Yet as she saw Stefano turn slowly around, his body tense and alert, she felt as if it wasn't.

She felt as if she'd asked something wrong. Something stupid.

'Allegra?' he queried softly, and she heard a stern note of warning in the sound of her name.

'I heard you…and Papa…' she whispered, wanting even now to explain, to understand. Yet the words trailed off as she saw Stefano's expression change, his eyes turning blank and hard, the mobile curve of his mouth flattening into an unforgiving line.

'Business, Allegra, business between men. It is nothing you need concern yourself with.'

'It sounded…' Her mouth was dry and she licked her lips. 'It sounded so…'

'So what?' Stefano challenged.

'Cold,' she whispered.

Stefano raised his eyebrows. 'What are you trying to say to me, Allegra? Are you having second thoughts?'

'No!' She grabbed for his hand and after a second he coolly withdrew it. 'Stefano…I just wondered…the things you said…'

'Do you doubt that I'll care for you? Protect and provide for you?' he demanded.

'No,' Allegra said quickly, 'but Stefano, I want more than that. I want—'

He shook his head with slow, final deliberation. 'What more is there?'

Allegra gazed at him with wide, startled eyes. *What more is there?* So much more, she wanted to say. There was kindness, respect, honesty. Sharing joy and laughter, as well as sorrow and heartache. Bearing one another's burdens in love. Yet she saw the hard lines of Stefano's face, the coldness of his eyes, and knew that he was not thinking of these things.

They didn't matter.

They didn't exist.

Allegra licked her lips. 'But Stefano…' she whispered, although she didn't know what to say. She barely knew what to feel.

Stefano held one hand up to stop her half-spoken plea. Something twisted his features, flickered in his eyes. Allegra didn't know what it was, but she didn't like it. When he finally spoke, his voice was calm, cold and frightening. 'Are you questioning what kind of man I am?'

His voice and face were so harsh, unfamiliar. Allegra shook her head. 'No!' she gasped, and it came out in a half sob for she knew then that she was. And so did he.

Stefano was silent for a long moment, his gaze hard and fastened on hers, until Allegra could bear it no longer and stared at the floor.

She realized he was treating her like a child—a child to be charmed or chastened, placated or punished.

With sudden, stark clarity, she realized he'd *always* treated her this way. She'd never felt like a wife, or even a woman.

She wondered if she ever would.

'Go to bed, Allegra.' He tucked a tendril of hair behind her ear, his thumb skimming her face once more. 'Go to bed, my little bride. Tomorrow is our wedding day. A new beginning, for both of us.'

'Yes…' she whispered. Except it didn't feel like a beginning. It felt like the end. Her throat was raw and aching and she couldn't look at him as she nodded. The implications of what he had said to her father—what he had now said to *her*—were flooding through her, an endless tide of confusion and fear. 'Yes…all right.'

'Do not be afraid.'

She nodded again, jerkily, as she moved backwards up the stairs. Stefano gazed up at her, his eyes burning into her mind, her heart, her soul. Burning and destroying.

She turned around and ran the rest of the way up.

'Allegra!'

Gasping aloud in frightened surprise, she saw her mother, Isabel, striding down the upstairs corridor. Allegra glanced behind her, but she could no longer see Stefano.

'What is the meaning of this?' Isabel demanded, belting her dressing gown, her long, still-blonde hair streaming behind her in a smooth ripple.

'I…I couldn't sleep.' Allegra stumbled into her bedroom and her mother followed. Everything was unchanged, she saw—the teddy bears, the tattered books, her wedding dress. All signs of her innocence, her ignorance.

'What is wrong?' Isabel asked. Her face, with its austere beauty, was harsh. 'You look as if you've seen a ghost!'

'Nothing is wrong,' Allegra lied quickly. 'I couldn't sleep and I went for a drink of water.'

Isabel arched one eyebrow and Allegra shrank back a little. She wasn't frightened of her mother, but she couldn't help but be nervous around her. After a lifetime of nannies and boarding school, she sometimes wondered if she even knew her mother at all.

Isabel's cold eyes swept over Allegra's dishevelled appearance. 'Have you seen Stefano?' she asked, and there was a sly note in her voice that made Allegra's skin crawl even as she shook her head.

'No. No, I—'

'Don't lie to me, Allegra.' Isabel took her daughter's chin in her hand, forcing her to remain still, as pinned as a butterfly uselessly fluttering its fragile wings. 'You never could lie to me,' Isabel said. 'You've seen him. But what's happened?' There was a cruel note in her voice as she added, 'Has the fairy tale been tarnished, my dear daughter?'

Allegra didn't know what her mother meant, but she didn't like her tone. Even so, she felt trapped, helpless. And alone.

And she wanted to confide in someone, anyone, even her mother.

'I saw him,' she whispered, blinking back tears.

There was a tiny pause that spoke far more than anything her mother could have said in words. 'And?'

'I heard him talking to Papa...' Allegra closed her eyes, shook her head.

Her mother exhaled impatiently. 'So?'

'It's all been a business arrangement!' This came out in a wretched whisper that caught on the jagged edge of her throat. Tears stung her eyes. 'Stefano never loved me.'

Her mother watched her with cool impassivity. 'Of course he didn't.'

Allegra's mouth dropped open as another illusion was ripped away. 'You knew? You knew all along...?' Yet even as she spoke the words, Allegra wondered why she was surprised. Her mother had never confided in her, never seemed to enjoy her company. Why shouldn't Isabel know? Why shouldn't she have been in on the sordid deal, the business of brokering a wife, selling a daughter?

'Oh, Allegra, you are such a child.' Isabel sounded weary rather than regretful. 'Of course I knew. Your father approached Stefano before your eighteenth birthday and suggested the match. Our social connections, his money. That was why he was at your party. That was why you *had* a party.'

'Just to meet him?'

'For him to meet you,' Isabel corrected coolly. 'To see if you were suitable. And you were.'

Allegra let out a wild laugh. 'I don't want to be suitable! I want to be loved!'

'Like Cinderella?' It would have been a taunt if her mother didn't sound so tired, so bitter. 'Like Snow White? Life is not a fairy tale, Allegra. It wasn't for me and it won't be for you.'

Allegra spun away, her hands scrubbing her face, bunching in her hair as if she could somehow yank the memory from her mind, forget the words Stefano had spoken to her father and then to her. Both conversations had damned him.

'It's not the Dark Ages, either,' she said, her voice trembling. 'You speak of this…this as if people can just barter brides…'

'For women like us, well-placed, wealthy, it is not so far,' Isabel returned grimly. 'Stefano seems like a good man. Be thankful.'

Seems, Allegra thought, but was he? She thought of the way he'd spoken to her father, the way he'd spoken to her, the coldness in his eyes, how he'd scolded and then dismissed her. *What more is there?*

She realized she didn't know him at all.

She never had.

'Honourable,' Isabel added, and now true bitterness twisted her words, her face. 'He has treated you well so far, hasn't he?' She paused. 'You could do worse.'

Allegra turned to stare at her mother, the cool beauty transformed for a moment by hatred and despair. She thought of her father's words, *I know a woman in Milan,* and inwardly shuddered.

'As you did?' she asked in a low voice.

Isabel shrugged, but her eyes were hard. 'Like you, I had no choice.'

'Papa spoke…Stefano said…things…'

'About other women?' Isabel guessed with a hard laugh. She shrugged. 'You'll be glad for it, in the end.'

Allegra's eyes widened. 'Never!'

'Trust me,' Isabel returned coldly.

Allegra was compelled to ask, her voice turning ragged, 'Have you *ever* been happy?'

Isabel shrugged again, closed her eyes for a moment. 'When the *bambinos* come…'

Yet her mother had never seemed to enjoy motherhood; Allegra was an only child and she'd been tended by nannies and governesses her whole life, until she'd gone to the convent school.

Would children—the hope of children—be enough to sustain *her* through a cold, loveless marriage? A marriage she had, only moments ago, believed to be the culmination of all her young hopes. Now she realized she had no idea what those hopes had truly been. They had been the thinnest vapour, as insubstantial as smoke. Gone now. Gone with the wind.

She thought of how she'd compared Stefano to Rhett Butler and she choked on a terrible, incredulous laugh.

'I can't do it.'

A crack reverberated through the air as her mother slapped her face. Allegra reeled in shock. She'd never been hit before.

'Allegra, you are getting married *tomorrow*.'

Allegra thought of the church, the guests, the food, the flowers. The expense.

She thought of Stefano.

'Mama, please,' she whispered, one hand pressed to her face, using an endearment she'd only spoken as a child. 'Don't make me.'

'You do not know what you're saying,' Isabel snapped. 'What can you do, Allegra? What have you been prepared to do besides marry and have children, plan menus and dress nicely? Hmm? Tell me!' Her mother's voice rose with fury. 'Tell me! What?'

Allegra stared at her mother, pale-faced and wild eyed. 'I don't have to be like you,' she whispered.

'Hah!' Isabel turned away, one shoulder hunched in disdain.

Allegra thought of Stefano's smooth words, the little gifts, and wondered if they'd all been calculated, all condescensions. *Not too bad a price.* He'd bought her. Like a cow, or a car. An object. An object to be used.

He hadn't cared what she thought, hadn't even cared to tell her the truth of their marriage, of his courtship, of *anything*.

Something hardened then, crystallised into cold comprehension inside her.

Now she knew what it was like to be a woman.

'I can't do it,' she said quietly, this time without trembling or fear. 'I won't.'

Her mother was silent for a long moment. Outside, a peal of womanly laughter, husky with promise, echoed through the night.

Allegra waited, held her breath, *hoped*...

Hoped for what? How could her mother, who barely cared for her or even noticed her at all, help her out of this predicament?

Yet still she waited. There was nothing else she could do, *knew* to do.

Finally Isabel turned around. 'It would destroy your father if this marriage fell through,' she said. There was a strange note of speculative satisfaction in her voice. Allegra chose to ignore it. 'Absolutely destroy him,' she added, and now the relish was obvious.

Allegra let her breath out slowly. 'I don't care,' she said in a low voice. 'He destroyed me by manipulating me—by giving me away!'

'And what of Stefano?' Isabel raised her eyebrows. 'He would be humiliated.'

Allegra bit her lip. She'd loved him. At least, she'd thought she did. Or had she simply been caught up in the fairy tale, just as her mother said?

Life wasn't like that. She knew that now.

'I don't want to create a spectacle,' she whispered. 'I want to go quietly.' She nibbled her lip, tried not to imagine the future ahead of her, looming large and unknowable. 'I could write him a letter, explaining. If you tell him tomorrow—tell Papa—'

'Yes,' Isabel agreed after a short, telling pause, her face a blank mask, 'I could do that.' Her eyes narrowed. 'Allegra, can you give this up? Your home, your friends, the life you've been groomed to lead? You won't be allowed back. I won't risk my own position for you.'

Allegra blinked at her mother's obvious and cold-hearted warning. She looked around her room. Suddenly everything seemed so beautiful, so precious. So fleeting. She sat hunched on her bed, hugging her old patched, pink teddy bear to her chest. In her mind she heard Stefano's voice, warm and confident.

Tomorrow is…a new beginning, for both of us.

Maybe she was wrong. Maybe she was overreacting. If she talked to Stefano, asked him…

Asked him what? The answer she'd been hoping for, *desperate* for, but he'd failed to give. He hadn't told her he loved her; he'd reprimanded her for asking the question in the first place.

There could be no future with him.

And yet what future was there for her without Stefano?

'I don't know what to do,' she whispered, her voice cracking. 'Mama, I don't *know*.' She looked up at her mother with wide, tear-filled eyes, expecting even now for Isabel to touch her, comfort her. Yet there was no comfort from her mother, just as there never had been. Her face looked as if it were carved from the coldest, whitest marble. Isabel gave a little impatient shrug. Allegra took a deep breath. 'What would you have done? If you'd had a choice back then? Would you still have married Papa?'

Her mother's eyes were hard, her mouth a grim line. 'No.'

Allegra jerked in surprise. 'Then it wasn't worth it, in the end? Even with children…*me*…'

'Nothing is worth more than your happiness,' Isabel stated, and Allegra shook her head in instinctive denial. She'd never heard her mother speak about happiness before. It had always been about duty. Family. Obedience.

'Do you really care about my happiness?' she asked, hearing the naked hope in her voice.

Her mother gazed at her steadily, coldly. 'Of course I do.'

'And you think…I'll be happier…'

'If you want love—' Isabel cut her off '—then yes. Stefano doesn't love you.'

Allegra recoiled at her mother's blunt words. Yet it was the truth, she knew, and she needed to hear it. 'But what will I do?' she whispered. 'Where will I go?'

'Leave that to me.' Her mother strode to her, took her by the shoulders. 'It will be difficult,' she said sternly, her eyes boring into hers, and Allegra, feeling as limp and lifeless as a doll, merely nodded. 'You would not be welcome in our house any longer. I could send you a little money, that is all.'

Allegra bit her lip, tasted blood, and nodded. Determination to act like a woman—to choose for herself—drove her to reckless agreement.

'I don't care.'

'My driver could take you to Milan,' Isabel continued, thinking fast. 'He would do that for me. From there a train to England. My brother George would help you at first, though not for long. After that…' Isabel spread her hands. Her eyes met Allegra's with mocking challenge. 'Can you do it?'

Allegra thought of her life so far, cosseted, protected, decided. She'd never gone anywhere alone, had no prospects, no plans, no abilities.

Slowly she returned the pink teddy bear to her bed, to her girlhood, and lifted her chin. 'Yes,' she said. 'I can.'

She packed a single bag with trembling hands while her mother watched, stony-faced, urging her on.

She faltered once when she glimpsed on her dressing table the earrings Stefano had given her the day before, to wear with her wedding gown.

They were diamond teardrops, antique and elegant, and he'd told her he couldn't wait to see her wearing them. Yet now she would never wear them.

'Am I doing the right thing?' she whispered, and Isabel leaned over and zipped up her bag.

'Of course you are,' she snapped. 'Allegra, if I thought you could be happy with Stefano, I would say stay. Marry him. See if you can make a good life for yourself. But you've never wanted a good life, have you? You want something great.' Her mother's smile was sardonic as she finished, 'The fairy tale.'

Allegra blinked back tears. 'Is that so wrong?'

Isabel shrugged. 'Not many people get the fairy tale. Now write something to Stefano, to explain.'

'I don't know what to say!'

'Tell him what you told me. You realized he didn't love you, and you weren't prepared to enter a loveless marriage.' Isabel reached for a pen and some lined notebook paper—childish paper—from Allegra's desk. She thrust the items at her daughter.

Dear Stefano, Allegra wrote in her careful, looping cursive. *I'm sorry but...* She paused. What could she say? How could she explain? She closed her eyes and two tears seeped out. 'I don't know what to do.'

'For heaven's sake, Allegra, you need to start acting like an adult!' Isabel plucked the pen from her fingers. 'Here, I'll tell you what to write.'

Isabel dictated every soulless word, while Allegra's tears splashed on to the paper and smeared the ink.

'Make sure he gets it,' she said as she handed the letter to her mother, scrubbing the tears from her eyes with one fist. 'Before the ceremony. So he's not...not...'

'I'll make sure.' Isabel tucked the letter in the pocket of her dressing gown. 'Now you should go. You can buy the ticket at the station. There's money in your handbag. You'll have to stay at a hotel for a night at least, until George returns.'

Allegra's eyes widened; she'd forgotten her uncle was staying in the villa. 'Why can't I just go with him?' she asked, only to have her mother tut impatiently.

'And how would that look? You can manage a hotel. I'll tell him tomorrow what's happened. They'll be back by the next day, no doubt. Now go, before someone sees you.'

Allegra gulped down a sudden howl of panic. She was so

afraid. At least marriage to Stefano had seemed familiar, safe. And yet, she asked herself, would it have been? Or would it have become the strangest, most dangerous thing of all—being married to a man who neither loved nor respected her?

Now she would never find out.

Isabel picked up the small bag that held nothing more than a few clothes, toiletries and keepsakes and thrust it at her daughter.

Allegra, now dressed in a pair of jeans and a jumper, clutched it to her chest.

'My driver is waiting outside. Make sure no one sees you.' Isabel gave her a little push, the closest she'd probably ever come to an embrace. 'Go!'

Allegra stumbled back to the door, then inched her way down the hallway. Her heart thudded so loudly she was sure the whole villa could hear it.

What was she doing? She felt like a naughty child sneaking out of bed, but it was so much more than that. So much worse.

She slipped on the stairs and had to grab on to the banister. Somewhere a floorboard creaked, and she could hear a distant sound of snoring.

She tiptoed down the rest of the stairs, across the slick terracotta tiles of the hall. Her hand was on the knob of the front door and she turned it, only to find it was locked.

Relief poured through her for a strange, split second; she couldn't get out. She couldn't *go*.

So she would go quietly back to bed and forget she'd ever had this mad, mad plan. She'd half-turned back when the door was unlocked from the outside. Alfonso, her mother's driver, stood there, tall, dark, and expressionless.

'This way, *signorina*,' he whispered.

Allegra glanced back longingly at her home, her life. She didn't want to leave it, yet she would have been leaving it all tomorrow anyway, and for a fate surely worse than this.

At least now she was in charge of her own destiny.

'Signorina?'

Allegra nodded, turning back from the warm light of her home. She followed Alfonso into the velvety darkness, her trainers crunching on the gravel drive.

Wordlessly, Alfonso opened the back door and Allegra slipped inside.

As the car pulled away, she gazed at her home one last time, cloaked in darkness. Her eyes roved over the climbing bougain-villea, the painted shutters, everything so wonderfully dear. In the upstairs window Isabel stood, her pale face visible between the gauzy curtains, and Allegra watched as her mother's mouth curved into a cold, cruel smile of triumph that made her own breath catch in her chest in frightened surprise.

Tears stinging her eyes, her heart bumping against her chest in fear, Allegra pressed back against the seat as the car moved slowly down the drive, away from the only home she'd ever known.

CHAPTER THREE

STEFANO WATCHED ALLEGRA stiffen, her fingers stilling on the buttons of her cheap coat. Her head was bent, her face in profile so he could see the smooth, perfect line of her cheek and jaw, a loose tendril of hair curling on to the vulnerable curve where her neck met her shoulder.

When he'd come here tonight—finagled an invitation all too easily from the ever striving Mason—he'd intended to speak to Allegra about business only. All he cared about was obtaining the best care for Lucio.

He didn't—wouldn't—care about the past, wouldn't care about Allegra. She was simply a means to an end.

Yet now he realized their history could not be so smoothly swept away. The past had to be dealt with…and quickly. Easily. Or at least appear as if it was.

He moved forward so his breath stirred that stray tendril of hair—as darkly golden as he remembered—and said, 'You're not leaving so early, are you?'

Slowly, carefully, she turned around. He saw her eyes widen, her pupils flare in shock as if, even now, after he'd spoken, she was surprised—afraid?—to see him there.

Stefano smiled and slipped the coat from her shoulders. 'It's been a long time,' he said. The memories, which pulsed between them with a thousand unnamed emotions, he firmly pushed to one side.

He saw Allegra gaze up at him, her eyes wide and luminous, reminding him so forcefully of the girl he'd known too many years ago. He felt a lightning streak of pain—or was it anger?—flash through him at that memory and he forced himself to smile.

All he could think about, care about, was Lucio. Not Allegra. Never Allegra. He let his smile linger as he asked, 'Won't you come into the party with me?'

It was bound to be a shock. Allegra knew that. Yet she still hadn't expected to be so affected, so aware. Of him.

Even now, she found herself taking in his appearance, her eyes roving almost hungrily over his form, the excellently cut Italian suit in navy silk, the lithe, lean strength of him, the utter ease and arrogance with which he stood, holding her coat between two fingers.

'Stefano,' she finally said, drawing herself up, bringing her scattered senses back into a coherent whole. 'Yes, it has been a long time. But I was actually just leaving.'

She'd envisiaged a scenario such as this many times—how could she not? Yet in each one she'd imagined Stefano furious, indifferent, or perhaps simply unrepentant. She'd never, in all of her imaginings, seen him smiling, looking like an old acquaintance who wanted nothing more than for them to catch up on each other's lives.

Yet perhaps that was precisely what they were. Seven years was a long time. Who knew how either of them had grown, changed? And Stefano had never really loved her in the first place; his heart hadn't been broken.

Not like hers had.

He hadn't given her her coat, she realized. He hadn't said a word, just smiled faintly in that aggravatingly arrogant way.

'My coat, please,' she said, trying not to sound annoyed, even though she was.

'Why are you leaving the party so early?' he asked. 'I've just arrived.'

'That may be, but I'm going,' she said firmly. She couldn't help but add, as curiosity compelled her, 'I didn't realize you knew my uncle's family that well.'

'Your uncle and I do business together.' His smile, still faint, now deepened. 'Did you not realize I'd been invited?'

'No,' she said shortly.

'From what I've gathered, your uncle and you are not on favourable terms.'

Allegra's gaze jerked up to his; he was staring at her with a quiet understanding that quite unnerved her.

'How do you know that?'

'I hear things. So do you, I imagine.'

'Not about you.'

'Then let me take this opportunity to fill you in,' he said, smiling easily. Too easily. Allegra shook her head in instinctive, mute denial.

She wasn't prepared for this. She'd expected to encounter hostility, hatred, or perhaps at worst—or at best—indifference.

Yet here he was, smiling, relaxed, acting like her friend.

And she didn't want to be his friend. She didn't want to be anything to him.

Why? Was she still angry? Did she still hate him? Had she ever hated him? The questions streaked through Allegra's mind like shooting stars and fell without answers.

'I don't think we really have anything to say to each other, Stefano,' Allegra said when she realized the silence had gone on too long, had become pregnant with meaning.

Stefano raised his eyebrows. 'Don't we?'

'I know a lot has passed between us,' Allegra said firmly, 'but it's all in the past now and I—'

'If it's in the past,' Stefano interjected smoothly, 'then it doesn't matter, surely? Can't we share an evening's conversation as friends, Allegra? I'd like to talk to you.'

She hesitated. Part of her howled inside that no, they couldn't, but a greater part realized that treating Stefano as a friend, an acquaintance, was the best way to prove to him, and to herself, that that was really all he was.

'It's been a long time,' he continued quietly. 'I don't know anyone here but George Mason, and I'd rather have more congenial company. Won't you talk with me for a while?' His smile twisted and the glint in his eyes was both knowing and sorrowful. 'Please?'

Again Allegra hesitated. All those years ago she'd left Stefano, left her entire life, because he'd broken her heart.

Yet now was her chance to show him, herself, the world, that he hadn't. Or, even if he had, she'd come out of the experience wiser, stronger, happier.

'All right,' she whispered. She cleared her throat and her voice came out stronger. 'All right, for a few minutes.'

His hand rested on the small of her back as he guided her back into the Orchid Room. Even though he was barely touching her, she burned from the mere knowledge of those fingers skimming the silk of her dress.

His touch. She'd once craved it, although in all of their engagement he'd never given her more than the barest brush of a brotherly kiss.

And now her body, treacherous as it was, still reacted to him, her senses screaming awake from the mere brush of his fingers.

At least she knew, Allegra told herself, and recognized it. At least she was aware of his power over her body. That, in itself, was power.

And after tonight, she would never see him again.

'Let me get you a drink,' he said as they entered the ballroom amidst a flurry of speculative looks and murmurs. 'What do you drink now? Not lemonade any more, is it?'

'No...' She found herself cringing at the memory of just what a child she'd been. 'I'll have a glass of white wine, dry, please.'

'Done.'

Allegra watched him disappear towards the bar and resisted

the urge to plunge back through the crowd, through the double doors, out of the hotel. Away from here…from him.

No, she needed this reckoning. Perhaps she'd been actually waiting for it, waiting for the day when she saw Stefano face to face and showed him that she was no longer the silly, star-struck girl who'd thought herself so lucky, so *blessed,* to have someone like him fall in love with her.

Just the memory of her own *naïveté,* of Stefano's deception, was enough to stiffen both her spine and her soul. Seeing him had been a shock; that was to be expected.

But she was different now, and she would show him just how different. How changed. They would have a drink for old times' sake, and then…

And then what?

Turning her back on the crowd, as well as the unfinished thought, she found another innocuous spot to station herself.

'There you are.' Stefano stood in front of her, two glasses of wine cradled in one hand, his smile wry. 'I thought you'd given me the slip.'

Allegra swallowed. Her throat felt too tight and dry to make any kind of reply. Given him the slip—as she had once before?

She reached for the glass of wine. 'Thank you.'

Stefano glanced at her, shrinking in the shadowy corner of the ballroom, and quirked one eyebrow. 'Why are you hiding, Allegra?'

'I'm not,' she defended herself quickly. 'This isn't exactly my crowd, that's all.'

'No? Tell me what your crowd is, then.' He paused before adding, 'Tell me about yourself.'

She glanced up at him, saw him looking down at her with that faint, cool smile that chilled her far more than it should. She found her own gaze sweeping over his features, roving over them, looking for changes. His hair was shorter and threads of silver glinted at his temples. His face was leaner, the lines of his jaw and chin more angular and pronounced. There was a new hardness in his eyes, deep down, like a mask over his soul. Or perhaps that had always been there and she hadn't known. She hadn't seen it, not until that last night.

'You're being rather friendly,' she said at last. 'I didn't expect it.'

Stefano rotated his wineglass between strong brown fingers. 'It's been a long time,' he said finally. 'Unlike your uncle, I try not to hold grudges.'

'Nor do I,' Allegra flashed, and Stefano smiled.

'So neither of us is angry, then.'

'No.' She wasn't angry; she just didn't know what she felt. What she was supposed to feel. Every word she spoke to Stefano was like probing a sore tooth to see how deep the decay had set in. She didn't feel the lightning streak of pain yet, but she was ready for it when it came.

Unless it never did. Unless she'd really healed her heart, moved on, just like she intended to show him. Just as she'd always told herself she had.

He took a sip of wine. 'So, what have you been up to these last few years?' he asked. Allegra suppressed the impulse to laugh, even though nothing felt remotely funny.

'I've been working here in London,' she finally said. She could feel him gazing at her, even though her own eyes were averted.

'What kind of work?' His voice was neutral, the carefully impersonal questions of an acquaintance, and for some reason that neutrality—that distance—stung her.

'I'm an art therapist.' He raised his eyebrows in question and Allegra continued, genuine enthusiasm entering her voice. 'It's a kind of therapy that uses art to help people, usually children, uncover their emotions. In times of trauma, expressing oneself through an artistic medium often helps unlock feelings and memories that have been suppressed.' She risked a glance upwards, expecting to see some kind of sceptical derision. Instead he looked merely thoughtful, his head cocked to one side.

'And you enjoy this? This art therapy?'

'Yes, it's very rewarding. And challenging. The opportunity to make a difference in a child's life is incredible, and I'm very thankful for it.' Her mouth was dry and she took another sip of cool wine. 'What about you?'

'I still own my company, Capozzi Electronica. I do less research now it has grown bigger. Sometimes I miss that.'

'Research,' Allegra repeated, and felt a surprising pang of shame to realize she'd never known he'd done any research at all. He'd never told her all those years ago, and she'd never asked. 'What kind of research?'

'Mostly mechanical. I develop new technology to improve the efficiency of industrial machinery.'

'You've lost me,' Allegra said with a little laugh and Stefano smiled.

'Most of it wouldn't concern your day-to-day living anyway. My research has been centred on machinery in the mining industry. A selective field.'

'Capozzi Electronica is a big business though,' Allegra said, 'isn't it? I've seen your logo on loads of things—CD players, mobile phones.'

Stefano shrugged. 'I've bought a few companies.'

She opened her mouth to ask another question, but Stefano plucked her wineglass from her fingers and gave her a teasing smile. 'Enough of that. The music is starting again and I'd like to dance. Dance with me?'

He held one hand out, just as he'd done all those years ago on her eighteenth birthday, when she'd walked down the stairs and into what she'd thought was her future.

Now she hesitated. 'Stefano, I don't think…'

'For old times' sake.'

'I don't want to remember old times.'

Stefano smiled faintly. 'No, neither do I, come to think of it. Then how about for new times' sake? New friendships.'

She stared at his hand, outstretched, waiting. The fingers were long and tapered, the skin smooth and tanned. 'Allegra?'

She knew this was a bad idea. She'd wanted to chat with Stefano like an old friend, but she didn't want to dance with him like one. Didn't know if she should get that close.

And yet something in her rebelled. Wanted to see how they were together, how she reacted to him. Wanted, strangely, to feel that lightning streak of pain…to see if it was there at all.

Mutely she nodded.

His hand encased—engulfed—hers and he led her on to the dance floor. She stood there woodenly, her feet shuffling in a parody of steps, while couples danced around them, some entwined, some holding themselves more awkwardly, all of them sliding her and Stefano speculative glances.

'This isn't a waltz, Allegra,' Stefano murmured and pulled her gently to him.

Their hips collided in an easy movement that was far too intimate…more intimate than anything that had passed between them during their engagement.

She felt the hard contours of him against her own softness, unyielding and strong. Allegra stiffened and jerked back even as her limbs went weak.

'I'm sorry,' she murmured, 'I don't dance that often.'

'Nor do I,' Stefano murmured back, his lips close—too close—to her hair. 'But I hear it's like riding a bike. You never forget.'

His arms were around her waist, his fingers splayed on her lower back. 'Do you remember how we danced? On your eighteenth birthday?' A glimmer of a smile lurked in the mobile curve of his mouth, although his eyes were shuttered. 'You clung to me for balance because you'd never worn heels before.'

Allegra shook her head, closed her eyes before snapping them open once more. 'I was a child.'

Stefano frowned, his eyes flickering across her face. 'Perhaps,' he said at last. 'But you aren't one now.'

'No,' Allegra agreed, 'I'm not.'

They danced in silence, swaying to the rhythm, their bodies—

chests, hips, thighs—all too tantalisingly close. Allegra felt herself relaxing, even though there was a taut wire of tension running through her core, vibrating with awareness.

She'd never expected it to happen like this. And yet, she realized, she'd expected to see Stefano again. A part of her, she acknowledged now, had been waiting for their reunion since the night she'd fled.

Why? she wondered, and her heart knew the answer. To show him how strong she was, how healed and healthy and happy she was…without him.

'What are you thinking?' Stefano murmured, and Allegra gazed at him through half-closed lids, soothed by the music and wine.

'How odd this is,' she admitted in a husky murmur. 'To be dancing with you…again.'

'It is odd,' Stefano agreed, his voice pitched low to match hers. 'But not unpleasant, surely.'

'I expected you to hate me.' Her eyes opened, widened. Waited.

He shrugged. 'Why should I, Allegra? It was a long time ago. You were young, afraid. You had your reasons. And, in the end, we didn't know each other very well, did we? A handful of dinners, a few kisses. That was all.'

Allegra nodded, accepting, though her throat was tight. He'd distilled their relationship down to its rather shallow essence, and yet it had been the most profound experience of her life.

'Do you hate me?' Stefano asked with surprising, easy candour. Allegra looked up, startled, and saw a shadow flicker through his eyes.

'No,' she said, and meant it. 'No. I've moved past it, Stefano.' She smiled, tried to keep her voice light. Breezy. 'It was a long time ago, as we've both agreed, and I've realized that you never lied to me. I just believed what I did because I wanted to.'

'And what did you believe?' Stefano asked softly. Allegra forced herself to meet his gaze directly.

'That you loved me…as much as I loved you.'

The words seemed to reverberate between them and for a strange second Allegra felt like the girl she'd been seven years ago, standing before Stefano and asking, *Do you love me?*

He'd never answered then, and he didn't now.

Allegra let out a breath. What had she expected? That he'd tell her he *had* loved her, that it had all been a mistake, a misunderstanding?

No, of course not. It hadn't been a mistake. It had been the right thing to do. For both of them.

Stefano hadn't loved her, hadn't even considered loving her, and she would have been miserable as his wife. She'd never regret her choice, never even look back. Not once. Not ever.

That you loved me…as much as I loved you. The words played a remorseless echo in Stefano's brain, even as he continued to dance, continued to feel Allegra's soft contours so tantalizingly close to him. He fought the urge to pull her closer, and closer still, and make her remember how they could have been all those years ago, if they'd been given the chance.

If she'd given him a chance.

But she hadn't, she'd made her decision that night, and he'd accepted it.

Hell, he'd made peace with it. Or at least he would now, for Lucio's sake.

Lucio… He forced his mind as well as other parts of his body away from Allegra's tempting softness and thought of his housekeeper's son, the grandson of the man who'd given him everything—shelter, food, opportunity—even at his own expense.

He wouldn't repay Matteo by neglecting his duty to his grandson. He wouldn't let Allegra distract him in his purpose… or, if it came to it, have him distract her.

His lips curved as he considered how many ways in which he could distract her…

No. No, the past was over. Finished.

Forgotten.

It had to be.

The music ended and they swayed to a stop before Stefano quite deliberately stepped away. It was time to tell Allegra the real reason why he was here…why he was dancing with her, or talking to her at all.

Allegra felt Stefano's arms fall away and resisted the urge to shiver. Out of the corner of her eye, she saw her uncle glowering and she looked away.

Stefano glanced around at the crowd of striving socialites and smiled. 'This crowd isn't really to my taste. What would you think about getting a drink some place more congenial?'

Allegra felt a leap of both anticipation and alarm in her chest. 'I don't…'

Stefano raised an eyebrow. 'Care to finish that sentence?' he asked dryly and Allegra realized she'd trailed off without knowing what to say. What to think.

What to feel.

'It's late,' she murmured, and wondered what she wanted Stefano to do. Take her reluctance as refusal or refuse to take no for an answer?

It galled her that she didn't know what she wanted him to do; she just wanted him to choose.

'It's not even ten o'clock yet,' Stefano said. There was a lazy lilt to his voice that made Allegra feel as if a purring cat had just leapt on to her lap. She wanted to stroke it, test its softness. 'One drink, Allegra. Then I'll let you go.'

'All right,' she said, her voice cautious, yet with not nearly as much reluctance as she knew she should have.

She wondered why she was reluctant, why she was afraid.

They'd just shown how grown up and civil they could be. The past was truly forgotten.

She wasn't that girl any more.

Stefano threaded her fingers with his own as he led her off the dance floor and away from the party.

This was strange, Allegra told herself as Stefano handed her her coat. Yet it was nice too, she realized as they headed out into the night, the September air cool on her flushed cheeks.

Too nice, perhaps.

'Where to?' Stefano stood on the kerb, an expensive woollen overcoat draped over one arm, his eyebrows raised in faint question.

'I'm afraid I don't know London nightspots very well.'

'Nor do I. But I do know a quiet wine bar near here that can be quite relaxing. How does that sound?'

'Fine. Lovely.'

She didn't see Stefano gesture to the doorman, but he must have for a cab pulled sleekly to a halt at the kerb. Stefano brushed the doorman aside and opened the car door himself, ushering Allegra in before he joined her.

Their thighs touched as he slid next to her, and Stefano did not move away. Allegra wasn't sure whether she liked the feel of his hard thigh pressing against hers or not, but she was certainly aware of it. Her hand curled around the door handle, nerves leaping to life.

They rode in silence, and Allegra was glad. She didn't feel up to making conversation.

After a few minutes, the cab pulled to a halt in front of an elegantly fronted establishment in Mayfair and Stefano paid the driver before he helped Allegra out. His hand was warm and dry and Allegra forced herself to let go.

She could not let herself be attracted to Stefano now. Not when she had a life, admittedly a small, humble one compared to his wealth and status, but one that was hers and hers alone.

Not when she knew what he was like. What he believed. Tonight was about being *friends*. That was all.

That was all it could be.

The wine bar was panelled in dark wood, with low tables and comfortable armchairs scattered around. It was like

entering someone's study and Allegra could see immediately
why Stefano liked it.

'Shall I order a bottle of red?' he asked, and Allegra bit her lip.

'I think I've had enough wine already.'

'What is an evening with friends without wine?' He smiled.
'Just drink a little if you prefer, but we must have a toast.'

'All right.' It did seem rather prim and stingy to sit sipping
iced water.

Stefano ordered and they were soon seated in two squashy
armchairs. Allegra even kicked off her heels—her feet had
been killing her—and tucked her legs up under her.

'So,' Stefano said, 'I want to hear more about what you've
been up to these last seven years.'

Allegra laughed. 'That's a rather tall order.'

He shrugged; she'd forgotten how wide his shoulders were,
how much power and grace the simplest of movements revealed.
'You're an art therapist, you said. How did that come about?'

'I took classes.'

'When you arrived in London?'

'Soon after.'

The waiter came with the wine and they were both silent
while he uncorked the bottle and poured. Stefano tasted it,
smiled and indicated for the waiter to pour for Allegra.

'*Cin cin,*' he said, raising his glass in the old informal toast that
reminded her of her childhood, and she smiled, raising her own.

She drank, grateful for the rich liquid that coated her throat
and burned in her belly. Despite Stefano's easy manner, Allegra
realized she was still feeling unsettled.

Seeing him brought back more memories than she'd ever
wanted to face. Memories and questions.

She had chosen not to face them when she'd left. She'd
quite deliberately put the memories in a box and unlike
Pandora, she'd had no curiosity to open it. No desire for the ac-
companying emotions and fears to come tumbling out.

When you didn't face something, she knew, it became easier

never to face it. It became quite wonderfully easy to simply ignore it. For ever.

Yet now that something was staring her straight in the face, smiling blandly.

Whatever Stefano had felt seven years ago, he'd clearly got over it. He'd put his ghosts, his demons to rest and had moved on.

And so had she.

Hadn't she?

Yes, she told herself, she had. She *had*.

Stefano crossed one long leg over the other, smiling easily. 'Tell me about these classes you took,' he said.

'What is there to tell?' Her voice came out too high, too strained. Allegra took a breath and let it out slowly. She even managed a laugh. 'I came to London and I lived at my uncle's house for…a little while. Then I got my own digs, my own job, and when I'd saved enough money I started taking night classes. Eventually I realized I enjoyed art and I specialised in art therapy. I received my preliminary qualification two years ago.'

Stefano nodded thoughtfully. 'You've done well for yourself,' he finally said. 'It must have been very difficult, starting out on your own.'

'No more difficult than the alternative,' Allegra retorted, and then felt a hectic flush sweep across her face and crawl up her throat as she realized the implication of what she'd said.

'The alternative,' Stefano replied musingly. He smiled wryly, but Allegra saw something flicker in his eyes. She didn't know what it was—hidden, shadowy—but it made her uneasy.

It made her wonder.

'By the alternative,' he continued, rotating his wineglass between lean brown fingers, 'you mean marrying me.'

Allegra took a deep breath. 'Yes. Stefano, marrying you would have destroyed me back then. My mother saved me that night she helped me run away.'

'And saved herself as well.'

Allegra bit her lip. 'Yes, I realize now she did it for her own ends, to shame my father. She used me as much as my father intended to use me.'

A month after her arrival in England, she'd heard of her mother's flagrant affair with Alfonso, the driver who had spirited Allegra away. Allegra had lost enough of her *naïveté* then to realize how her mother had manipulated her daughter's confused and frightened state for her own ends—the ultimate shaming of the man she despised, the man who had arranged Allegra's marriage.

Her husband.

And what had it gained her?

By the time Isabel had left, Roberto Avesti was bankrupt and his business, Avesti International, ruined. Isabel hadn't realized the depth of her husband's disgrace, or the fact that it would mean she would be, if not broken-hearted, then at least broke.

Allegra bit her lip, her mind and heart sliding away from that line of conversation, those memories, the cost her own freedom had demanded from everyone involved.

'Even so,' she said firmly, 'it's the truth. I was nineteen, a child, I didn't know who I was or what I wanted.'

Stefano's face was expressionless, his eyes blank, steady on hers. 'I could have helped you with that.'

'No, you couldn't. Wouldn't.' Allegra shook her head. 'What you wanted in a wife wasn't—isn't—the person I was meant to become. I had to discover that for myself. Back then I didn't even know I was missing anything. I thought I was the luckiest girl in the world.' Her voice rang out bitterly.

'And something made you realize you weren't,' Stefano finished lightly. 'I know it shocked you to realize our marriage was arranged, Allegra, as a matter of business between your father and me.'

'Yes,' she agreed, 'it did. But it wasn't just that, you know.'

Stefano cocked his head, his eyes alert. 'No? What was it, then?' His voice was bland and mildly curious yet Allegra still felt a strange *frisson* of fear. Unease.

Suspicion.

'You didn't love me,' Allegra said, striving to keep her voice steady. 'Not the way I wanted to be loved, anyway.' She shrugged. 'It doesn't matter now, does it?' she said, trying to keep her voice light. 'It's all past, as you said.'

'Indeed.' Stefano's voice was chilly, the expression in his eyes remote at best. 'Still,' he continued, his voice thawing, turning mild, 'it must have been difficult for you to set up a new life here, leave your family, your home.' He paused. 'You've never been back really, have you?'

'I've been to Milan, for professional reasons,' Allegra replied, hearing the defensive edge to her voice.

Stefano shrugged in dismissal. 'But you have not been home.'

'And where's home, exactly?' Allegra asked. 'My family's villa was auctioned off when my father declared bankruptcy. My mother lives mostly in Milan. I don't *have* a home, Stefano.' Her voice rang out clear and sharp, and she looked down, wanting to recover her composure, wishing it hadn't been lost.

She didn't want to talk about her family, her home, all the things she'd lost in that desperate flight. She didn't want to remember.

'Is London your home?' Stefano asked curiously, when the tense silence between them had gone on too long. Too long for Allegra's comfort, at any rate.

She shrugged. 'It's a place, as good as any, and I enjoy my job.'

'This art therapy.'

'Yes.'

'And what of friends?' He paused, his fingers tightening imperceptibly on his wineglass. 'Lovers?'

Allegra felt a *frisson* of pure feeling shiver up her spine. 'That's not your business,' she said stiffly and he smiled.

'I only meant to ask, do you have a social life?'

She thought of her handful of work acquaintances and shrugged again. 'Enough.' Then, since she wasn't enjoying this endless scrutiny, she asked, 'And what of you?'

Stefano raised his eyebrows. 'What of me?'

Suddenly she wished she hadn't asked. Wasn't sure she wanted to know. 'Friends?' she forced out. 'Lovers?'

'Enough,' Stefano replied, a faint feral smile stealing over his features. 'Although no lovers.'

This admission both startled and pleased her. Stefano was so virile, so potent, so utterly and unalterably male that she would have assumed he had lovers. *Loads.*

Probably he only meant he had no lovers currently, Allegra thought cynically. No arm candy for the moment, none for this evening.

Except her.

He was with *her* tonight.

'Does that please you?' Stefano asked, breaking into her thoughts and making her gaze jerk upwards in surprise.

'It doesn't matter,' she countered swiftly.

'No, of course not, and why should it?' Stefano's smile turned twisted, cynical. 'Just as it doesn't matter to me.'

Allegra nodded, uncertain. Of course, the words were right, yet the tone wasn't. The feeling wasn't.

She saw something spark in Stefano's eyes, something alive and angry, and she set her wineglass on the table. 'Perhaps this was a bad idea. I was hoping we could be friends, even if just for an evening, but maybe, even after all this time, we can't. I know memories can hurt. And hurts run deep.'

Stefano leaned forward, his fingers curling around her wrist, staying her.

'I'm not hurt,' he said, his voice quiet and firm, and Allegra met his eyes.

'No,' she said, suddenly, strangely stung, 'you wouldn't be, would you? The only thing that was hurt that day was your pride.'

His eyes glinted gold, burned into hers. 'What are you saying?'

'That you never loved me.' She took a breath and forced herself to continue. 'You just *bought* me.'

He shook his head slowly. 'So you claimed in that letter of yours, I remember.'

Allegra thought of that letter, with its girlish looping hand-writing and splotchy tear-stains and felt the sting of humiliation.

He wasn't even denying it, but it hardly mattered now.

'I think I should go,' she said in a low voice and Stefano released her, leaning back in his chair. 'I never meant to bring all this up, talk about it again.' She tried to smile, even to laugh, and wasn't quite able to. 'Perhaps it would have been better if I'd left before you came into the party. If we hadn't seen each other at all. We almost missed each other, as it was.'

Stefano watched her, smiled faintly. 'That,' he said, 'wasn't going to happen.'

Allegra felt a lurch of trepidation, as if everything had shifted subtly, suddenly. 'What do you mean?'

'We weren't going to miss each other this evening, Allegra,' Stefano said with cool, calm certainty. 'I came to the party—to London—to see you.'

CHAPTER FOUR

'ME?'

Stefano watched the emotions chase across Allegra's features: shock, fear, pleasure. He smiled. Even now, she wanted his attention. His touch.

And he couldn't stop touching her, whether it was her back as he'd steered her through a crowded ballroom, or her thigh in the darkened confines of a city cab. He was drawn to her, despite both his desire and intent to the contrary. He wanted to touch and to know the woman he'd once believed he could love.

Love. *You never loved me.* How many times had she told him now, he wondered cynically. How many times had she thrown it in his face? No, he hadn't loved her, not the way she'd wanted. Not like Galahad, Rhett Butler, or whatever ridiculous caricature of a man she'd imprinted in her childish mind.

It hardly mattered now anyway. Love was not the issue; Lucio was.

He smiled, broke the silence. 'Yes, you,' he said.

Allegra blinked. Stared. She heard a buzzing in her ears. Felt it in her soul. 'What do you mean?' she finally said, though she'd heard what he'd said. She just couldn't believe it.

'I knew you would be at this wedding, and I wangled an invitation from your uncle. It wasn't difficult. He was thrilled to be getting such a notable guest.' His lips curved in a mocking smile that had Allegra gritting her teeth at his unshakeable arrogance.

'Why?' she whispered. 'Why did you want to see me, Stefano?'

Stefano cradled his wineglass between his hands, staring into its ruby contents before he raised his head. His expression was stony, bleak. 'Because I've been told you're the best art therapist for children in this country.'

Allegra jerked back, startled. She hadn't expected *that*. What, a mocking little voice asked, did you expect? For him to declare that he'd missed you? *Loved* you?

'I think that's overstating the case rather a lot,' she said after a moment. 'I've only been qualified for two years.'

'The doctor I spoke to in Milan recommended you unreservedly.'

'Renaldo Speri,' Allegra guessed. 'We corresponded regarding a case I had, a boy who had been misdiagnosed with autism.'

'And he wasn't autistic?'

'No, he was severely traumatised from witnessing his mother's suicide.' She grimaced in memory. 'It was a remarkable breakthrough, but I can't really take the credit for it. Anyone could have—'

'Speri thinks highly of you,' Stefano said with a shrug. 'He seems to think you're the best. And I want the best.'

Allegra watched him for a moment. The best. So she was a commodity, a possession. Just as she'd been all those years before. Would Stefano ever think of her otherwise? Did he even know how?

At least the difference now, she thought cynically, was that the arrangement was mutual.

'Why didn't you tell me this when we first met, Stefano? Why come to the reception at all?' Why ask her to dance, take her for a drink, talk about *lovers?*

She shook her head, felt a tide of humiliation wash over her at the realization of how Stefano had been manipulating her…as he had before. Softening her up for the request. The kill.

She felt another wave of humiliation crash over her as she

remembered her own thoughts, the pleasure she'd felt at believing Stefano wanted to be with her. Treacherous, half-acknowledged desires that Stefano had undoubtedly surmised. She closed her eyes briefly, sickened by his deception, and by herself for falling for it…again.

She opened her eyes and met Stefano's blank gaze with a stern one of her own. 'If you were interested in me professionally, you should have come to my office, made an appointment—'

Stefano shrugged, unrepentant. His face was expressionless, yet his eyes blazed into hers. 'You know it's not as simple as that, Allegra. The past still lies between us. I needed to see how things would be between us. If we would be able to work together.'

'And can we?' she asked, eyebrows raised, her voice sharpened with both sarcasm and curiosity.

'Yes.' He spoke flatly, with cold certainty. 'We can.' He leaned forward, his eyes intent on hers, trapping her with his unrelenting gaze. 'The past is forgotten, Allegra.'

Yet it hadn't felt forgotten a moment ago, Allegra thought, suppressing a shiver of unease. That flash of something dark and primal in Stefano's eyes had made her feel as if it wasn't forgotten at all.

'And for this you needed to ask me to dance? Invite me out for a drink?' She shook her head. 'If you want me to help you, Stefano, help whatever child you are thinking of, then you need to be honest with me. From the beginning. I won't abide liars.'

Stefano's eyes narrowed. 'I am not a liar,' he said coldly. 'How was I not honest, Allegra? We had a past. I wanted to make sure it wouldn't interfere with what I am proposing before I set it before you. That's all.'

She pressed her lips together against a useless retort…a *revealing* retort. There was nothing Stefano had done, she acknowledged silently, that she could point her finger at. Accuse him of. Yet she was still cross, still *hurt,* and she still felt uneasy, uncertain. Uncomfortable.

'All right, fine,' she said at last. 'Why don't you tell me what exactly you're proposing?'

Stefano paused. 'The hour's late,' he said. 'And it's been a long evening. Why don't we talk about it another time? Tomorrow, perhaps? Over dinner?'

Allegra frowned. 'Why not Monday, in my office?' she countered.

'Because I'll be back in Rome on Monday,' Stefano replied with firm finality. 'Allegra, I am interested in you only as a professional—'

'I know that!' she said, a flush rising to her cheeks.

'Then why not converse over dinner? We've just shown how we can be reasonable this evening. We can even, perhaps, be friends.' He smiled, his amber eyes glinting with a promise Allegra remembered all too well. A promise of tenderness and compassion, of understanding and caring. Of love.

False. All false.

Allegra took a breath. Stefano was right; she *was* letting the past cloud the present issue, which was presumably a hurting child.

She had to forget it, had to move on as she knew she'd done all those years ago. Yet seeing Stefano had brought it rushing back.

She lifted her chin. 'All right. Tomorrow.'

'Tell me your address and I'll fetch you.'

'There's no need—'

'I'll fetch you,' Stefano repeated. He didn't raise his voice, didn't need to. He simply smiled. Smiled and waited.

Allegra chose to capitulate gracefully. Some battles, she knew, were not worth fighting. Not yet.

She gave it to him, then rose from her chair. He stood also. 'Goodnight, Stefano,' she said, and she held out her hand.

He glanced down at it, smiling wryly, before he took it in his. Her hand felt so small in his, small and fragile.

'Good night, Allegra,' Stefano said, his voice a husky murmur. 'Until tomorrow.'

* * *

All the next day Allegra's mind hurtled from alarm to anticipation, marking quite a few assumptions along that perilous mental route.

Stefano wanted to contract her services as an art therapist for a child. A *child*.

His child?

His wife?

She probed these possibilities with careful, clinical precision. Did it hurt? How much pain?

She wasn't jealous, she knew that. She wasn't even that surprised. So what did she feel?

She didn't know. Couldn't answer. More thoughts, more emotions to tuck away in that box.

As day darkened into twilight, Allegra surveyed the slim pickings of her wardrobe.

She'd splurged on the dress for Daphne's party, and there was nothing else remotely as sophisticated or expensive in her wardrobe. Her work clothes were generally plain and comfortable, and the few dresses she had were stodgy and serviceable.

Allegra sighed. Why hadn't she considered this before? She'd have had the time, if not the money, to buy something at the shops.

Why, that objectionable little voice whispered inside her, do you care? Are you trying to impress him? *Attract* him?

'No,' Allegra said aloud but, even alone in her bedroom, her voice sounded flat and false.

With a growl of impatience, she turned to the rack of clothes and picked a dress out at random. It was an olive green coat dress that she'd bought on sale for an interview, and while it presented a reliable if rather depressing image for work, it was hardly something one wore to dinner…especially if that dinner was at one of London's classiest restaurants, which Allegra had no doubt it would be, knowing Stefano.

Knowing Stefano… Did she really know him?

Seven years was a long time for both of them. She'd never have expected him to act as he had last night, putting the past behind them. Wanting to be her friend. Caring about what she thought.

And the only reason he'd done those things, she reminded herself, was because he wanted something from her.

She slipped on the coat dress, only to grimace in rueful dismay at her reflection. She looked awful, drab and dreary, and she was vain enough to want to look at least half-decent for Stefano.

Not beautiful, not sexy, not alluring. But attractive, at least. Attractive and professional, confident and calm.

She chose a pair of slim-fitting black trousers and a white silk blouse that was plain but well-tailored.

Catching her hair up in a chignon—nothing careless about it this time—she nodded at the rather austere image she presented. Professional, puritanical.

'For the best,' she reminded herself. After all, she was having dinner with Stefano in her professional capacity, not personal. Nothing personal. Nothing *ever* personal.

The intercom for the front door sounded, and Allegra hurried to buzz him through.

The walls were so thin, she could hear the creak of the stairs and his tread down the hall and her heart started to hammer.

She grabbed her coat and handbag and met him in the hallway.

'Thanks for coming,' she said quickly. 'I'm ready.'

Stefano raised an eyebrow. He looked devastating in a charcoal-coloured suit, a crisp white shirt and mulberry-coloured silk tie. 'We could have a drink first.'

'Let's go out,' Allegra suggested. 'My flat's tiny.' She realized with a little pang of shame that she didn't want him to see her poky flat with its second-hand furnishings. Art therapists, even ones who'd had significant successes, didn't make much money.

She was proud of her flat, but she knew it would seem pathetic to him—the little life she'd built for herself—compared with what he had. What he'd been prepared to offer her.

Stefano made no comment, merely shrugged one shoulder

before gesturing for her to lead the way down the cramped hallway.

Out in the street, traffic blared along with the stereo systems propped in windows, and there was an overwhelming smell of greasy kebab on the air.

Allegra smiled brightly. 'Where to? We could walk…'

Stupid, she told herself. Stefano would have made reservations at a place far from here.

'I have a car.' He gestured to a black luxury car idling at the kerb. A few passers-by were giving it curious—and envious—looks as the driver hopped out and opened the back door for them.

'I hope you don't mind…?' Stefano asked politely. 'If you wanted to eat more locally—'

'No,' Allegra hastened to assure him, 'this is fine.'

It was more than fine. It was amazing. She'd spent the last seven years in severely squeezed circumstances and she'd forgotten that this was the kind of life she'd once been accustomed to. The kind of life Stefano had always known.

'Thank you for giving me a lift,' she said stiffly as the car pulled away from the kerb. 'I could have taken a cab, met you at the restaurant.'

'Yes,' Stefano agreed, his voice pleasant and mild, 'you could have.'

Allegra was conscious of the enclosed space, the forced intimacy of their shared seat, thighs and shoulders brushing, touching. She sneaked a glance at Stefano, saw the clean, strong lines of his cheek, his jaw, and curled her fingers into a fist in her lap.

'So why don't you tell me about the child in need of therapy?' she said after a moment when the only sounds had been the muted traffic from outside and their own breathing.

'Let's wait until we get to the restaurant,' Stefano replied. 'Then we won't be interrupted.'

Allegra nodded. It made sense, but the silence that stretched between them was unnerving, and she didn't even know why.

This wasn't personal, she reminded herself. It was professional. Stefano was nothing more than another parent in desperate need of help for his child. As long as she remembered that…

'Allegra,' Stefano said softly. He smiled as he put one large hand on her leg. Her thigh. Allegra stared down at his fingers, tense, transfixed. 'Relax.'

She realized how tense she was, coiled tightly, ready to strike or to flee. She smiled, tried to laugh, tried to relax, and failed at both. 'I'm sorry, Stefano. This is just a bit strange for me.'

He smiled, his gaze flickering over her features. 'Me too.'

'Is it?' she asked frankly, and his smile deepened.

'Of course. But what's important now, what has to be important, is Lucio.'

'Lucio,' Allegra repeated. His son. 'Tell me about him.'

'I will, soon.' He gazed down at his own hand, her leg, as if suddenly aware of what he had done. How he'd touched her.

He didn't move his hand, and the confines of the car suddenly seemed airless, tiny. Allegra couldn't remember how to breathe. He has a son, she told herself, which means he has a wife.

Finally, with a little smile, he removed his hand and Allegra drew in a lungful of air. Had he always affected her that way, she wondered hazily, or was it new?

Whatever it was, it didn't matter. It wouldn't.

They rode in silence for a quarter of an hour before the car pulled up to a luxury hotel on Piccadilly.

Stefano ushered her up the steps and through the doors and then, surprisingly, to a lift. They rode up in silence and when the lift doors opened Allegra gave a little gasp of pleasure, for they were at the top of the hotel and beyond the elegantly set tables and tall glass vases of creamy lilies, the whole of London's skyline stretched enticingly to the dark horizon, spangled with lights, glittering with promise.

A waiter ushered them to the most private table, tucked in an alcove with long windows on either side of them. Allegra sat down, felt the weight of the heavy linen napkin as the waiter placed it in her lap.

'Is this all right?' Stefano asked and she smiled mischievously.

'I suppose it will have to do.'

Stefano smiled back, his eyes glinting in the dim light, and for a moment they seemed complicit in their own little joke, their own world. It caused Allegra's heart to skip two beats and a bubble of laughter to well up in her throat.

She felt the cares and worries that had been tightening like an iron band around her heart ease. They very nearly slipped away altogether and she let them go, even gave them a little push.

This could work, she told herself. It was working. They were interacting in a professional way, friendly and relaxed. Just as it should be.

Allegra took a sip of water. 'Tell me, do you come to London often?'

'Occasionally on business,' Stefano replied, 'although mainly I've been doing business in Belgium.'

'Belgium? What's there?'

He gave a little shrug. 'That industrial machinery I told you about. Mining industry.' He smiled faintly. 'Very boring.'

'Not to you, I suppose.'

'No,' he agreed, his expression darkening as if a shadow had passed briefly over him, 'not to me.'

'I don't even know what made you interested in that,' Allegra acknowledged ruefully. 'I feel like I actually know very little about you.' When they'd met all those years ago, he'd asked her questions about herself. She'd been happy to chatter on about all of her silly, girlish interests. He'd been happy to listen. She winced now at the memory.

And what had she known of him? He was from Rome; he owned his own company; he was rich and handsome and he had wanted her.

Or so she'd thought…until she'd realized that all he'd wanted was her social status, her family's standing.

Not her, never her.

'I suppose I thought you knew what was important,' Stefano replied.

'Like what?'

'That I'd protect and provide for you,' Stefano replied. He spoke calmly, easily even, and yet Allegra felt chilled.

He was the same, she realized with a sickening stab of disappointed longing. Protection. Provision. Those were what had mattered, what still mattered. Not love, respect, honesty, or even common interests, shared joys. Just the careful handling of an object. A possession…something bought and paid for. That wasn't love, she thought, wondering why it mattered. Why she cared. That kind of love wasn't real. It was worthless.

Why should she have thought—*hoped*—he'd changed? That kind of belief was the bedrock of a man's soul. It didn't change. It didn't even crumble.

'Yes,' she murmured, taking another sip of water to ease the sudden dryness of her throat, 'I knew that.'

'Why don't we look at the menu?' Stefano suggested and there was a knowing gleam in his eye. Allegra had no doubt that he'd realized how dangerously deep the waters swirling between them had become, and he was steering them to safer, shallower eddies.

She glanced down at the menu, the elegant gold script, half of it in French, and swallowed a laugh.

Stefano glanced at her over the top of his menu. 'You learned French in school, didn't you?'

Allegra thought of the convent, the lessons she'd learned there. Silence. Submission. Subservience. 'Schoolgirl stuff,' she dismissed with a little smile, and stared back down at her menu. 'What are langoustines?'

'Lobster.'

'Oh.' She gave a little grimace; she'd never liked seafood. Stefano chuckled softly. 'Perhaps we should have gone somewhere a bit less international.' He perused the wine menu, adding carelessly, 'You seem to have become rather English.'

Allegra didn't know why she felt stung, except that it sounded like an insult. 'I am half English,' she reminded him and he glanced up at her, his eyes dark, fathomless.

'Yes, but the girl I knew was Italian to her core…or so I thought.'

Allegra put down her menu. 'I thought we agreed that we didn't know each other very well back then. And anyway, we're different people now.'

'Absolutely.' Stefano put down his own menu. 'Have you decided?'

'Yes. I'll have the steak.'

'And to start?'

'The herb salad.' She pressed her lips together, because she knew he was going to order for her and it irritated her. Another way of providing, she thought sardonically, gazing out of the window.

The waiter, aware of the precise second they'd put down their menus, came to the table.

As Allegra had thought, Stefano ordered for both of them.

'How would madam like the steak done?'

Stefano began to speak and Allegra interjected frostily, '*Mademoiselle* would like it medium rare.'

There was a moment of surprised silence and Allegra realized she'd just spoken like a child.

Acted like one.

Felt like one.

Why did Stefano do that to her? she wondered wearily. Why did she allow him to? Even now, when she was here as a professional, when he wanted her for her expert services?

'If you wanted to order for yourself,' Stefano said mildly once the waiter had gone, 'you could have told me.'

'It doesn't matter,' Allegra dismissed firmly, although Stefano still looked unconvinced. 'Why don't we talk about Lucio now?' she suggested. No more raking up the past, the memories swirling about like fallen leaves around them. 'He's your son?'

Stefano looked genuinely startled. 'No, he's not. I don't have a son, Allegra.' He paused, and she thought she saw something flicker in his eyes—that darkness again, a glimpse of his soul. Then he continued, 'I'm not married.'

'I see.' She took a sip of water and tried to frame her thoughts. Her feelings. Relief was the overwhelming emotion, and on its heels came annoyance for she'd no business being relieved about Stefano's single status. 'I just assumed,' she explained. 'Most adults who come to me are the parents of the child in question.'

'Understandable,' Stefano replied, 'and in truth Lucio is like a son to me. A nephew, at the very least. His mother, Bianca, is my housekeeper.'

And mistress? Allegra wondered. She pressed her lips together to stop herself from voicing her suspicion aloud, knowing just how petty and petulant she would sound. 'I see.'

Stefano smiled although there was a hardness in his eyes. 'You probably see quite a lot that isn't there,' he replied, and Allegra blushed. 'But, in fact, Lucio and Bianca are like family to me. Bianca's father, Matteo…' He stopped, shrugged. 'The relevant details are that Lucio's father, Enzo, died nine months ago in a tractor accident. He was the groundskeeper for my villa in Abruzzo. After his death, Lucio began to lose his speech. Within a month of the accident he stopped speaking completely. He hasn't…' He paused, his expression darkening, eyes shadowed with painful memory.

'He's retreated into his own world,' Allegra surmised softly. 'I've seen it before, when children experience a sudden and severe trauma. Sometimes the easiest way of coping is by not coping at all. Just existing without feeling.'

'Yes,' Stefano said, and Allegra heard ragged relief in his voice. 'That's just what he's done. No one can reach him, not even his own mother. He doesn't cry, doesn't throw tantrums…' He shrugged helplessly, hands spread wide. 'He doesn't do anything, or even seem to feel anything.'

Allegra nodded. 'And you've tried therapies before this, I presume? If this has been going on for nine months?'

'He's been evaluated,' Stefano explained heavily. 'Although not as quickly as he should have been.' Regret turned his voice harsh. 'At the time of his father's accident, Lucio wasn't even four years old. He was a quiet boy as it was, and so his condition went undetected. Bianca had taken him to a grief counsellor, who said that some withdrawal was a normal sign of grieving.' Stefano's head was bowed and Allegra felt a tightening pang of sympathy for him and his situation. It was so familiar from her work, but it always hurt. Always.

'Then,' Stefano continued, 'as he began to lose speech, develop certain behaviours, the counsellor recommended he be evaluated. When he was, he was diagnosed with pervasive developmental disorder.'

'Autism,' Allegra finished quietly and Stefano nodded. 'What types of behaviours was he exhibiting?'

'You can look at his case notes, of course, but the most obvious one was lack of speech or eye contact. Methodical, or repetitive, play. Abnormal level of sustained concentration, resistance to cuddling or physical contact.' Stefano recited the litany of symptoms in a flat voice and Allegra could imagine how he—and Lucio's mother—had felt when they'd heard the doctor. No one wanted to hear the news that their child was flawed in some way, especially when the problems associated with autism were not easily treated.

The waiter came with their first courses and they spent a few moments eating, both grateful for the slight respite. When their plates had been cleared, Stefano continued.

'He was first diagnosed with autism a few months ago but Bianca resisted. She felt certain that Lucio's behaviour stemmed from grief rather than a disorder, and I feel the same way.'

Allegra took a sip of water. 'I presume it has been explained to you,' she said gently, 'that the symptoms associated with autism often manifest themselves at Lucio's age.'

'Yes, of course, but right around the time his father died? It's too much of a coincidence.'

'It also doesn't make sense for Lucio to lose speech and develop other worrisome behaviours months after a trauma,' Allegra countered, her voice steady and quiet. 'Especially at such a young age.'

'Are you trying to tell me you think he's autistic?' Stefano demanded.

'It's a possibility,' Allegra replied. 'A misdiagnosis among professionals is rare, Stefano. Psychiatrists aren't just slapping a label on a child without care or reason. They draw on extensive evaluation and data—'

'I thought you'd had experience with a child who was misdiagnosed,' Stefano replied coolly.

'Yes, one. One child in hundreds, thousands. And it simply happened that he responded to art therapy, and I happened to be his art therapist.' She shook her head. 'I'm not a miracle worker, Stefano. If you want to hire me to prove Lucio isn't autistic, then I can give you no guarantees.'

'I don't expect guarantees,' Stefano replied. 'If, after extensive work, you come to the same conclusion as the other medical professionals, then Bianca and I will have no choice but to accept it. However, before that time, I want to give Lucio another chance to heal. For the last several months, the doctors involved have been treating him for autism. What if his real problem is grief?' He lifted his bleak gaze to meet hers and Allegra felt a wave of something unfamiliar, something tender, sweep over her.

'It is possible,' she allowed, 'and I couldn't really say any more until I saw his case notes. Why do you think art therapy in particular might help Lucio?'

'He always loved to draw,' Stefano said with a little smile. 'I have a dozen thirty-second masterpieces by my desk. And while I'll admit I was sceptical with the idea of creative therapy—' he shrugged, his mouth quirking cynically '—at this point, I'm willing to try anything. Especially when I heard about your success with a similar case.'

'I see.' She appreciated his honesty, and it was no more than what most parents initially expressed. 'So Lucio lives in Abruzzo?'

'Yes, and I won't move him. Bianca had to take him out of nursery because he couldn't abide strange places any more. Regular trips to Milan or further afield would not be possible.'

'So,' Allegra surmised slowly, 'you need an art therapist— me—to come to Abruzzo.'

'Yes, to live there,' Stefano completed without a flicker. 'For at least a few months initially, but ideally…' he paused '…as long as it takes.'

He poured them both wine from the bottle the waiter had uncorked and left on the side of the table. Allegra took a sip, letting the velvety-smooth liquid coat her throat and burn in her belly.

Several months in Abruzzo. With Stefano.

Professional.

'That's quite a commitment,' she said at last.

'Yes. I imagine you have some cases you'd need to deal with, business that would have to be wrapped up. I'm returning to London in a fortnight. You could be ready by then?' There was a slight lilt to his voice, but Allegra knew it wasn't really a question.

Stefano wasn't even *asking* her to come to Abruzzo. He was expecting her. Telling her.

As high-handed as ever, she thought. As arrogant and pre-sumptuous as he'd been when he'd patted her on the head and told her to go to bed.

Dream of me.

What more is there?

She shook her head, a tiny movement, but one Stefano still noticed. 'Allegra?' he queried softly. 'Two weeks surely is enough to do what you need to do here?'

Questions clamoured in her throat. 'What if I can't come to Abruzzo, Stefano?' she asked, and heard the needling challenge in her voice. 'What if I say no?'

Stefano was silent, his eyes blazing into hers for a long, heated moment. 'I didn't think,' he said finally, quietly, enunciating every syllable with chilling precision, 'that you would allow the past, our past, to threaten the future of an innocent child.'

Allegra's face flushed with anger. 'This isn't about the past, Stefano! It's about the present, and my professional life. I'm not your star-struck little fiancée to order about at will. I'm a qualified therapist, a *professional* you are seeking to contract.' She broke off, letting her breath out sharply.

An all too knowing smile flickered across Stefano's face and died. 'Are you sure it's not about the past, Allegra?' he asked softly, and at that moment Allegra wasn't.

Their second courses arrived, and she looked down at her succulent steak with absolutely no appetite.

'Let's eat,' Stefano suggested. 'You can take the time to consider any more questions you might have regarding this situation. I'm happy to answer them.'

'Will you be in Abruzzo for the entire time?' Allegra asked abruptly. Stefano stilled, and she felt exposed, as if she'd revealed something too intimate by that simple question.

Perhaps she had.

'No,' he answered after a moment. 'I'll divide my time between Abruzzo and Rome. You'll deal mostly with Lucio's mother, Bianca, although, of course, I will continue to take an interest.'

'I see.' Relief and disappointment coursed through her, each emotion irritating in its complexity.

They ate then and Allegra found, a bit to her annoyance, that her appetite had returned and the steak was delicious.

By the time their meal was finished, she felt her calm, cool, impersonal demeanour return. She was grateful for it; it gave her armour. 'I'll need to see Lucio's case notes, of course,' she said as the waiter took their plates. 'And speak to Dr Speri, and anyone else who has interacted with him.'

'Of course.'

Allegra glanced at Stefano and saw, despite his carefully
neutral expression, the hope in the brightness of his eyes, the
determined, drawn line of his mouth. 'I'm not a miracle worker,
Stefano,' she reminded him gently. 'I may be no help at all. As
I said before, you have to contend with the possibility that
Lucio is indeed autistic.'

A muscle bunched in Stefano's jaw and he gave a little
shrug. 'Just do your job, Allegra,' he said, 'and I'll do mine.'

Allegra nodded, slightly stung by his tone, although she
knew she shouldn't be. 'I'll need a few days to look over all
the material on Lucio's case,' she said after a moment. 'I'll let
you know my decision by the end of this week.'

'Wednesday.'

She wanted to protest, felt a cry clamour up her throat,
straight from her gut, her heart. She wanted to tell him he
couldn't order her around her any more, that she knew—she
knew what kind of man he was.

Yet she pressed her lips against such useless retorts. The past
was forgotten. She just seemed to keep having to forget it.

Besides, Stefano's behaviour was only that of a concerned
adult. He wanted answers, and he wanted them quickly.

'Wednesday,' she repeated with a small, brisk nod. 'I'll do
my best, Stefano, but there is no point rushing me. You're
asking a lot of me, you realize, to give up my entire life in
London for an extended period—'

'I thought you'd appreciate a professional challenge,'
Stefano countered. 'And a few months is hardly a long time,
Allegra. It's not seven years.'

She glanced at him sharply, wondering what he meant by such
a comment. She didn't feel like asking. She didn't want to fight.

'Even so, this is a decision which should be considered carefully on both sides. As you reminded me yourself, it's Lucio
we have to consider foremost.'

'Of course.' He spoke as if it were assumed, automatic. As
if he hadn't considered anything else, hadn't for one second

been caught up in the emotions that Allegra felt swirling around and through her, making her think, wonder.

Remember.

'Will you be having dessert?' The waiter had come to their table, and they ordered dessert, a chocolate gateau for Stefano and a sticky toffee pudding for her. When the waiter had gone and the menus were cleared Stefano faced her again, brisk and businesslike.

'I'll ring you on Wednesday, then.'

'Yes, fine.' Allegra licked her lips, felt the deepening pang of doubt. 'Stefano, perhaps you should consider another art therapist. There are plenty available, and even though the past is forgotten, it still exists.' She toyed with her fork, unable to quite meet his eyes as she confessed quietly, 'It could be difficult at times for both of us.'

Stefano was silent long enough for Allegra to look up and meet his knowing gaze.

'There isn't another art therapist who has the experience you do,' he replied, his tone flat and final. 'One who is also Italian, who has the ability and willingness to spend several months in a rather remote place.'

'You're assuming rather a lot—' Allegra interjected and Stefano smiled, although it was a gesture tinged with sorrow.

'Am I? The girl I knew would have done anything—gone anywhere—to help someone in need. But perhaps you've changed.'

'It's not that simple, Stefano,' Allegra replied. She wouldn't be manipulated or emotionally blackmailed. She wouldn't let Stefano use those tactics on her. Not now. Not again.

'It never is,' he agreed, and Allegra was silent.

Their desserts came and Stefano turned the conversation to easier topics—films, the weather, London's sights. Allegra was relieved to talk without considering how every word she said might be interpreted, and what every rejoinder of Stefano's might mean.

It was quite late in the evening when they finally left the restaurant. Stefano's car was waiting as they left the hotel, and Allegra wondered how he did that.

Had Stefano rung the driver? Had the driver waited there the whole evening? How did everything come so easily to people in power?

Except, perhaps, where it mattered. She thought of Lucio, and how much he obviously meant to Stefano, with a compassionate pang.

They drove back to Allegra's flat in virtual silence. Allegra didn't know if she was imagining the heavy expectancy of that silence, as if something had already been decided.

As if something was going to happen.

A light, misting rain was falling, softening the street into a grey haze, as Stefano pulled up to Allegra's building.

'You don't have to come in,' Allegra protested vainly, for Stefano was already through the front door.

'I'll see you safely to your door,' he said, but there was nothing safe about his presence, filling up the tiny hallway. He was too big for the space, she thought, too *much*. He towered over her, near her.

'It's perfectly safe,' she protested and Stefano just smiled. He was gazing at her, that familiar glint in his amber eyes, a spark Allegra knew could become a fully-fledged blaze. She swallowed, pressing against the wall as if she could put some distance between them.

'Stefano…' she began, and then stopped because she didn't know what else to say.

'I wondered what it would be like, when I saw you again,' Stefano said. His voice was pitched low, a husky murmur that still managed to make Allegra tremble.

'I have too, of course,' she said, and tried to keep her voice light, friendly. She failed.

'I wondered if you would be the same,' Stefano continued. He lifted his hand as if to touch her and Allegra held her breath.

'I wondered,' he continued, his voice turning huskier, 'if you would look at me the same way.'

'We're different, Stefano,' Allegra said. She wished she could tear her eyes away from his burning gaze, wished she could keep her body—and perhaps even her heart—from reacting. Wanting. 'I'm different,' she added, but it was no deterrent. He smiled, his fingers touching her cheek, tucking a tendril of hair behind her ear.

'Yes,' he murmured, 'you are.'

The light touch of his fingers was enough to send sensation spiralling through her. Enough to make her dizzy, to close her eyes. She snapped them open.

'Don't do this, Stefano,' she whispered. She didn't have the will power to pull away and it shamed her. 'You're hiring me in a professional capacity. You shouldn't do this.'

'I know I shouldn't,' Stefano agreed, but there was no regret in his voice, only decision.

He was moving closer, his body inches from hers—chest, torso, stomach, thighs. She felt his heat come off him in intoxicating waves and she took a deep, gulping breath.

'We should say goodnight,' she managed, her voice turning breathless because suddenly it seemed as if there was no air in the hallway, no air in her lungs. Her body was transfixed, her eyes on his, watching his lids lower, his lashes sweep his cheeks and still he moved closer. 'We should shake hands,' she added desperately, for she knew it wasn't going to happen.

Something else was.

'We should,' Stefano agreed. His fingers drifted down her cheek, traced the full outline of her lips. His fingers left a trail of tiny shocks along her skin and Allegra forced herself to remain still, not to lean into his hand, into *him,* because at that moment she wanted nothing more.

'Of course,' Stefano continued, 'we could seal a business deal with a kiss.'

'That's not how I do business,' she countered, choking on air.

'Don't you want to know, Allegra?' he whispered, his lips a

scant inch from hers. 'Don't you want to know how it is between us…how it could have been, for all these years?'

She tried to shake her head, tried to frame a word, a thought. Why was it so hard to think? Her mind was as misty as the evening outside, her thoughts evaporating into haze.

Then his lips came down on hers, a mere brush turning into something hard, demanding, a possessive brand.

Mine.

His.

Allegra realized dimly in the last cogent part of her brain that Stefano had never, not even remotely, kissed her like this before. The kisses they'd shared all those years ago had been chaste pecks, brotherly brushes, and she'd thought those had sent a spark spiralling through her body!

This kiss turned her to fire.

His mouth moved on hers, his tongue tasting, testing and finding.

Her arms came up around his shoulders and she revelled in the sheer size and power of him, her hands bunching on his arms, her nails digging into his skin.

Stefano's arms came around her, holding and supporting her for Allegra realized she'd sagged bonelessly against him, needing his strength.

When he finally lifted his mouth from hers, his arms still around her, she had not a single thing to say. To think.

The feelings blazing through her were simply too much.

'Sealed with a kiss,' he whispered in satisfaction and stepped back. 'I'll ring you on Wednesday,' he promised. 'But now I'll leave you to your dreams.'

Dream of me.

'Goodnight, Allegra.'

Wordlessly she nodded, watched him open the door and disappear into the drizzle. In the shattered silence of the hallway she let out a choked gasp, a half-laugh, her mind and heart seething with both confusion and unfulfilled desire.

She touched her fingers to her lips as if she could still feel
him there, his sure possession, and thought numbly that the past
was *not* forgotten.

As his car pulled away from the kerb, Stefano could still see
Allegra in the hallway. She sagged against the wall, one hand
touching her lips, and he smiled—smiled with a hard satisfaction that settled in him, through him, with savage pleasure.

She wanted him. Just as before. Perhaps, he thought
musingly, more.

She wanted him, even though she didn't want to, even
though she denied it. Denied it to him as well as to herself.

And yet that kiss, wonderful as it was, had been a mistake.
He couldn't afford to tangle with Allegra, for Lucio's sake as
well as his own.

Wouldn't.

He'd been down that road once before, knew where it ended,
and it was nowhere he wanted to be.

He leaned his head against the back of the seat and closed
his eyes. He'd kissed Allegra because he'd wanted to; he'd
wanted to feel her lips under his, her body against his. He'd
wanted to discover if the reality lived up to his dreams.

And did it? he wondered with a cynical smile.

Perhaps, but it didn't matter. He wasn't going to kiss
Allegra again.

She was Lucio's therapist, nothing more.

Never, he told himself savagely, anything more again.

CHAPTER FIVE

WEDNESDAY AFTERNOON FOUND Allegra in her office, Lucio's case notes scattered on her desk. She gazed unseeingly out of the window at a dank, grey London sky and waited for Stefano's call.

She'd been quite determined, after that shocking, *shattering* kiss, not to take Lucio's case. The personal conflict was obvious and overwhelming.

There were plenty of other art therapists, she told herself. Ones who were more experienced as well as not personally involved.

Yet was she personally involved? Her mind staunchly said no, but the rest of her, her body still remembering that tide of desire, spoke differently.

Yet she wanted to take the case, she realized. She was professional enough to separate any feelings for Stefano from her work with Lucio, and she wanted to help this boy whose case notes spoke of a tragic, silent eight months. She wanted to help him for his own sake as well as for her own.

The idea of working intensively with one child for a prolonged period of time was inspiring, exciting. No more forty-five minute slots while parents waited, desperate for her to have made a difference.

No endless slog of case after case without hope or happiness.

She wanted this change, this chance.

Even if Stefano was involved.

Especially if Stefano was involved.

For while this could be an opportunity with Lucio, it was also an opportunity to put the past to rest. Redeem it, even.

And show Stefano, once and for all, that she was not that girl any more, the girl he thought he knew, the girl who'd loved him.

The phone trilled, startling Allegra out of her thoughts. She picked it up.

'Hello?'

'Allegra.' It sounded like a caress somehow, even though his voice was brisk. 'You've seen Lucio's case notes?'

'Yes.'

There was a moment of pulsing silence and Allegra realized how hard her heart was beating.

'And?'

'Yes, I'll take the case, Stefano. Although…'

'You have some reservations.'

'Yes.'

'Because of our kiss the other night.' He spoke steadily, without apology or concern, yet Allegra found her hand gripping the telephone receiver far too tightly.

'Yes,' she said after a moment of tense silence. 'Stefano, as we've said, I'm coming to Abruzzo in a professional capacity. There can't be—'

'There won't.'

She blinked, swallowed, strangely, stupidly stung that he sounded so certain. 'Even so,' she forced herself to continue, 'I don't want there to be any…tension…because of what has happened between us. It would be best for Lucio, as well as for ourselves, if we could be friends.'

'Then we will be.'

Allegra gave a shaky laugh, for she knew it wasn't that simple, and surely Stefano knew it as well. You couldn't will yourself into being friends; you couldn't will feelings or memories to disappear.

You could just put them in a box.

'You never kissed me like that when we were engaged,' she

blurted, and then wished she hadn't. Stefano was silent although she could hear him breathing.

'You were nineteen,' he finally said, his voice flat. 'A child, as you pointed out to me. I was taking my time with you, Allegra.' He paused, she waited. 'You weren't, however, a child last night. But have no fear. It's an incident that will not be repeated.'

He spoke so firmly and finally that Allegra was left with nothing left to do but accept.

'All right, then,' she finally said. She knew there was no point trawling old ground over the telephone.

'I'm flying to London next Friday,' Stefano said. 'That should give you time to hand off any cases, and you can return to Rome with me. From there we'll go to Abruzzo.'

'All right.'

'Email me with anything you'll need for your work,' Stefano said, 'and I'll arrange for it to be there when you arrive.'

'Fine…'

He gave her his email address and then, when the only thing left to say was goodbye, he surprised her.

'Allegra,' he said. 'Thank you.'

'You're welcome,' Allegra said. 'I'm looking forward to it, Stefano. I want to help Lucio.'

'So do I.'

More silence, and Allegra longed to say something, but she didn't know what it was. What did you say to someone you'd been planning on spending the rest of your life with? Having his children?

Loving him?

What did you say to someone who had never loved you back, who had planned to marry you for your name and your status and nothing else?

What did you say to someone who had broken your heart?

'Goodbye,' she finally said quietly, and put down the telephone.

In the end, it was remarkably easy to hand off her few cases. Since she freelanced, her work wasn't permanent anyway, and within a week she'd cleared her desk, sublet her flat and packed two suitcases with the things she thought she'd need.

It was strange and a bit disturbing to realize how easily she'd dismantled her life, a life she'd built with her own sweat and tears over the last seven years. None of it had been easy, and yet now, for the present, it was gone.

It was a cloudy day in mid-September, the leaves drifting down in lazy circles under a wispy blue sky, when Stefano arranged to pick her up.

Allegra waited outside since it was warm, felt nerves leap to life as she gazed down Camberwell Road for the first sign of Stefano's luxurious black car.

When it finally pulled sleekly into view, she was calm, focussed on the firm purpose of her journey and its destination.

Stefano exited the car. He was dressed in a dark suit, a mobile phone pressed to his ear, and his manner was so abrupt and impersonal that any anxiety Allegra had felt about seeing him again since their kiss trickled shamefacedly away.

At the moment, he looked as if he didn't even remember her, much less their kiss. She wondered if he'd spared it a moment's thought, while she'd given it several hours' confused contemplation.

Stefano was still on his phone as the driver put her bags in the boot and Allegra climbed into the car.

They pulled away from her street, her home, her life, and Stefano hadn't even said hello.

Twenty minutes into their journey, Stefano finally finished his conversation.

'I apologise,' he said. 'It was a business call.'

'So it would seem.'

He smiled, his eyes glinting with a rare humour. 'I told Bianca about your arrival, and she's looking forward to meeting you. You're providing a new hope for all of us, Allegra.'

Allegra nodded. 'Just remember there are no guarantees, no promises.'

'No, but there aren't with anything in life, are there?' He spoke lightly, yet Allegra heard an undercurrent of bitterness, saw it flash across his face. Was he referring to something else? Their own disappointed dreams?

She gave herself a little shake and gazed out of the window as they came on to the motorway. She had to stop reading innuendo and remembrance into every word Stefano said.

The past was *forgotten*.

It felt like a prayer.

They took a private jet to Rome. Allegra realized she should have expected no less, yet the blatant, if understated, display of Stefano's wealth and power awed her.

'Are you richer now than seven years ago?' she asked curiously when they were seated on the plane, the leather seats huge and luxurious.

Stefano glanced at her over the edge of his newspaper. 'A bit.'

'I know my father was wealthy,' Allegra said, 'but, to tell you the truth, I don't feel I saw much of it.'

'You were comfortable?' Stefano asked, his eyebrows raised, and Allegra laughed.

'Yes, of course. Trust me, I'm not giving you some poor little rich girl story.' She shrugged. 'I just saw very little of life, and I think that's why I was so swept away when I met you.'

'I see.' His voice was neutral, betraying no indication of agreement.

Allegra gazed out of the window. The plane was rising above the grey fog that covered London and a bright, hard blue sky stretched endlessly around them.

She had a strange urge to talk about the past, even though she knew there was no point, no purpose. She wanted to exorcise it, to show Stefano how little it mattered, how utterly *over* it she was.

It was a childish impulse, she knew, and worse, she wasn't even sure if she could pull it off.

Yet what was there to talk about? What was there to say, that hadn't been said that night?

Do you love me?

What more is there?

Even if their marriage hadn't been a business arrangement, Allegra knew, it wouldn't have been a good match. It wouldn't have made her happy. Stefano hadn't loved her, not in a real or worthwhile way. He'd only thought of her as a possession, something to be protected and provided for, tucked on a shelf. Taken care of.

Nothing else, nothing equal or giving or real about it.

And he'd shown her in a thousand tiny ways since then that he was the same. Thought the same, loved the same, which really wasn't love at all.

Worthless.

Allegra turned back to Stefano. He was reading the paper, his head bent, his legs crossed.

'You have a flat in Rome,' she said. 'Which part?'

He glanced up, smiling at her faintly, the glint in his eyes making Allegra feel as if he were simply humouring her. 'Parioli, near the Villa Borghese.'

'I've never actually been to Rome,' she admitted, a bit embarrassed by her own inexperience. Her life in Italy had consisted of home and convent school, summers at their villa by the lake, and nothing more.

'I'd show you the sights, if we had the time,' Stefano said.

'We'll leave for Abruzzo right away?'

'Tomorrow. I have a business dinner tonight. A social occasion.' He paused, his gaze sliding away from hers. 'Perhaps you would care to come with me.'

Allegra stiffened, felt the confusion of conflicting emotions. Alarm, surprise, pleasure. 'Why?' she asked. Her question was blunt but necessary.

Stefano raised his eyebrows. 'Why not? Most people bring dates and I don't have one.'

'I'm not a date.'

'No, you're not,' he agreed, unruffled, unconcerned. 'But you're with me, and there's no point in you staying alone in the villa, is there?' He smiled again, humour flashing briefly in his eyes. 'I thought we were supposed to be friends.'

'We are,' she said quickly. 'It's just—'

Eyebrows still raised, Stefano waited. Allegra realized he'd tangled her up in her own words. Yes, she wanted them to be friends, and therefore these innocent, innocuous occasions should provoke no alarm or anxiety. And yet…

And yet they did. They did, because they weren't just friends. No matter how much she wanted to dismiss their kiss, their entire past, she couldn't. Not as much as she wanted to.

And yet she couldn't avoid it. Perhaps the only way across this swamp of memory and feeling, Allegra thought, was straight through. It might mean getting muddy, wet, dirty, and even hurt, but she couldn't avoid Stefano, or what was and had been between them. She didn't even want to.

The past, forgotten as it might be, had to be dealt with. Directly.

'All right,' she said, and gave a little nod. 'Thank you. That should be…' she sought for a safe word and finally settled on '…pleasant.'

'Pleasant,' Stefano repeated musingly. He turned back to his paper. 'Yes. Indeed.'

She turned back to the window.

They didn't talk again until the jet landed at Rome's Fuimicino airport, and Stefano helped her from the plane.

The air wrapped around her like a blanket—dry, hot, familiar. Comforting.

Home.

She took a breath, let it flood through her body, her senses. The air was different here, the light brighter.

Everything felt different.

'It's been a long time,' Stefano said, watching her, and Allegra shrugged.

'Six years.'

'You came back for your father's funeral.'

'Yes.' They were walking across the tarmac to the entrance to customs, and Allegra kept her head averted. Her father's funeral. Her father's suicide. More things she chose not to think about. To remember.

'I'm sorry about his death,' Stefano said after a moment, his voice quiet and far too understanding.

Allegra shrugged. When she spoke, her voice sounded as hard and bright as the sky shimmering above them. 'Thank you. It was a long time ago.'

'The death of a parent still hurts,' Stefano replied, his gaze searching hers, and Allegra shrugged again and looked away.

'I don't really think of it,' she said, and felt as if she'd revealed something—had exposed it to Stefano's unrelenting gaze, unrelenting *knowledge*—simply by making that throw-away comment.

Mercifully Stefano dropped the subject and they spent the next short while dealing with customs and immigration.

Stefano had all of their papers in order and it didn't take long. All too soon they were pulling away in yet another hired car, the ocean a stretch of blue behind them, the flat, dusty plains in front and the scattered brown hills of Rome against the horizon.

Allegra felt exhaustion crash over her in a numbing wave. She'd been physically busy these last few weeks but, more to the point, emotionally she'd been in complete overdrive. She leaned her head against the leather seat and closed her eyes.

She didn't realize she'd actually dozed until Stefano nudged her awake. The sedan had pulled to a stop in front of a narrow street of elegant town houses, all with painted shutters and wrought iron railings.

'We're here,' Stefano murmured, and helped her from the car. Allegra followed him into the town house. It was elegantly decorated with antiques, sumptuous carpets and priceless paintings, yet it did not have the stamp of individuality on it, of Stefano.

It was impossible, Allegra thought even as she admired what looked like a Picasso original, to know anything about the person who lived here except for the fact that he was fabulously wealthy.

She wondered if Stefano wanted it that way. She was realising, more and more, that she'd never really known him when they'd been engaged. She'd thought that before, of course, when she'd overheard that terrible conversation with her father. Yet now she thought of it in a different, more intimate way, a way that wasn't fraught with anger and hurt, only a certain sorrowful regret.

She wanted to ask him what books he liked, what made him laugh. The things she should have known and delighted in when she'd been his almost-bride.

And she wouldn't ask those questions, she told herself sternly, wouldn't even *think* of asking them, because there was no point. *Professional.*

'I know you're tired,' Stefano said, 'and you can rest upstairs if you like. I'll have the cook prepare something light for lunch.'

'Thank you.' Allegra hesitated. 'The dinner tonight…I assume it's a formal occasion?'

'Yes.'

'I don't have anything appropriate to wear, I'm afraid,' Allegra said. She kept her voice light, even though she felt embarrassed. 'Evening gowns aren't usually required in my line of work.'

Stefano gazed at her, his face expressionless, yet Allegra saw—sensed—a flicker of something in his eyes. She wished she knew what he was thinking, wished she could ask.

He gave a brief nod. 'I'll send someone to the shops to select something for you. Unless you'd prefer to go yourself?'

Allegra shook her head. She wouldn't know what to choose, and just the thought of wandering around Rome by herself exhausted her.

'Very well. I need to attend to business, but Anna, my house-keeper, will show you your room.'

As if on cue, a kindly, slight, grey-haired woman emerged from the back corridor.

'This way, *signorina,*' she said quietly in Italian.

'*Grazie,*' Allegra murmured, and the language—her native tongue—felt strange to her ears. She'd spoken English, only English, for years.

Had it been a deliberate choice? A way to forget the past, harden her heart against who she was?

A way to become the person she was now—the English Allegra, Allegra the art therapist. Not Allegra who had stood at the bottom of the stairs, her heart in her eyes for all to see.

She followed Anna up thickly carpeted stairs to a beautifully appointed bedroom. Allegra took in the wide double bed with its rose silk cover, the matching curtains, the antique walnut chairs flanking a marble fireplace. It was far finer than anything she'd ever known, even in her father's villa.

She smiled at Anna. '*Grazie,*' she said again and Anna nodded and left.

Allegra sank onto the bed, overwhelmed and overawed. Even though it was only early afternoon, she stripped off her clothes and slipped beneath the cool, smooth sheets.

She could hardly credit that she was here, in Stefano's house, in Stefano's bed…one of them, anyway. She laughed aloud, but the sound held no humour. Alone in the huge bedroom, it sounded lonely. Little.

Allegra closed her eyes. Emotions had been flickering through her since she'd first seen Stefano again, flickering to life after seven years of numbness, and she was tired of them, tired of feeling. She didn't want to analyse how she felt, what she thought, what Stefano felt or thought.

She just wanted to *be.* To do her job, as Stefano had told her to. She hoped, when she finally met Lucio, she could forget about Stefano completely…

On that hazy thought, sleep overtook her.

She woke to a light knock on the door as late afternoon sunlight slanted across the floor.

'Allegra?' Stefano called softly. 'You've been asleep for four hours. We need to get ready for the dinner.'

'I'm sorry,' she mumbled, pushing a tangle of hair from her eyes. Stefano opened the door and Allegra was conscious of her dishevelled appearance, the fact that, even with the coverlet held up to her chest, it was quite obvious she was wearing only a bra and panties.

Stefano's gaze swept over her for one blazing second, and Allegra felt an answering awareness fire her nerve endings, turn her breathless.

Then his face blanked and he gave her a polite, impersonal smile. 'There is a selection of evening gowns for you to choose from downstairs. I'll bring them up.'

'A selection?' Allegra repeated in surprise, but Stefano had already gone.

Allegra took the opportunity to slip out of bed and throw on the clothes she'd left discarded on the floor. She was just tying her hair back when he reappeared a few moments later with several elegantly embossed carrier bags.

'Everything you need should be in there,' he said. 'We need to leave in a little under an hour. Anna is going to bring you up some antipasti. You missed lunch.' He smiled briefly, a teasing, affectionate look in his eyes that did something strange—something pleasant—to Allegra's insides.

'Thank you,' she managed, 'for being so thoughtful.'

He inclined his head. 'You're welcome.'

It was a simple exchange, almost meaningless, and yet, as Stefano left, closing the door behind him, Allegra realized she'd enjoyed it. She liked things simple. She liked not wondering what the hidden meaning or feeling was.

She wanted to enjoy. Enjoy an evening playing dress up like a little girl let loose in her mother's wardrobe.

Smiling at the thought, Allegra reached for the carrier bags.

Stefano had provided everything—three different designer gowns, all with matching shoes and wraps, as well as undergarments and tights.

She let the silky, luxurious fabrics slide through her fingers. She hadn't had such beautiful clothes in seven years. Hadn't needed them and certainly hadn't been able to afford them.

She was touched by Stefano's thoughtfulness, even though she knew it was simply his way of operating. She was in his care, so he would provide for her. Everything, always, whether she liked it or not.

She chose a slim-fitting knee-length gown in taupe silk. It was simple yet elegant and clearly well made. She liked the way the silk rippled over her, smoothing to a silhouette as she tugged up the zip.

In the bottom of one of the bags, Stefano had left a small velvet box and when Allegra opened it she let out a small shocked gasp.

They were the earrings he'd given to her the day before the wedding. The earrings he'd told her he couldn't wait to see her wearing. The earrings she'd never worn, just as there had been so many things she'd never done.

She slipped them from their velvet bed, saw the way the lamplight glinted off their myriad facets, and blinked back tears.

She didn't know why she felt like crying; she couldn't untangle the way she felt. Yet, at that moment, she didn't feel like a possession—she felt like a treasure.

This was dangerous, she knew. Dangerous to let herself feel this way, to flirt on the blurred edge of friendship. It would be far safer to keep her distance from Stefano, to maintain that professional facade.

Yet at this moment, beautifully dressed and about to embark on an evening of entertainment, she didn't want to.

At this moment, she wanted to be treasured.

She slipped the earrings on and left her hair down, tumbling over her shoulders.

Then she went downstairs.

Stefano was already in the marble hallway, dressed in a tuxedo. He quite literally took her breath away as he turned to face her, his eyes glittering with honest admiration when he saw her.

'You look stunning,' he said, and there was nothing but simple sincerity in his voice. His eyes rested on her ears, the diamond teardrops sparkling against her skin, and he smiled, an intimate gesture that spoke more than any word.

Allegra realized she was smiling back, glowing as if she'd swallowed the sun. As if Stefano had handed it to her.

'Thank you.'

He held out his hand and Allegra took it with only a second's hesitation. She wasn't going to let herself think too much. This was one evening, one evening only, and she planned to enjoy it.

They took a car to the St Regis Grand Hotel. As they pulled up to the hotel's front, Allegra couldn't help but be impressed by its ornate facade. They were in the heart of Rome, minutes from the Spanish Steps and the Trevi Fountain, worldly, witty people moving, talking and laughing all around them along with the trill of mobile phones and the hum of mopeds.

And Allegra was a part of it. She *felt* a part of it.

The mid-September air was a balmy caress as they climbed the steps to the hotel. As they entered, Allegra was struck by the huge chandelier suspended glittering above them, the tinkling music from a grand piano, the marble columns and sumptuous carpets that almost caught her heels, all conspiring to create an overwhelming sense of luxury and privilege.

Stefano guided her into the Sala Ritz, yet another sumptuous room decorated with marble pillars soaring to a ceiling with hand-painted frescoes and possessing the same aura of accustomed wealth. Businessmen and their well appointed wives mingled among black-frocked waiters bearing trays of champagne.

Allegra saw the heads turn as Stefano moved through the room, one hand on the small of her back. She saw the eyes slide speculatively towards her, heard the silent questions.

She shook her hair back and smiled proudly. Possessively.

Stefano joined a small group of men and introduced Allegra to his associates.

'Gentlemen, my friend, Allegra Avesti.'

My friend. Something she'd never been to him before. And she wondered now, distantly, if that was what she really was. If she *could* be that to Stefano. If she wanted to be.

Yet what other choice was there?

She watched surprise flicker across their faces as they heard the words *my friend.* A few jaws dropped, and Allegra wondered why they were so surprised.

Surely Stefano had come to business occasions with a woman before—a woman who was not a steady girlfriend or perhaps even a date.

Or was it something else? Unease prickled uncomfortably through her, up her spine and along her insides. Was it that he did come to these functions with a woman, a particular woman, and she was not that woman?

There was no time to consider such a question, or how it had made her feel, as she was soon swept up in the pre-dinner conversation, and took comfort in the innocuous chatter.

'All right?' Stefano murmured, his hand holding her elbow, and Allegra felt his breath graze her cheek, felt her whole body shiver at the touch and sound of him.

'Yes,' she murmured back, 'I'm all right. Enjoying myself, actually.'

'Good.' There was a note of possessive satisfaction in his voice that should have alarmed her, should have reminded her that Stefano simply thought of her as an acquisition, and a recent one at that. Services purchased and rendered.

But she didn't want to think, didn't even want to feel, at least not too much. She just wanted to enjoy. So she smiled lightly and let Stefano guide her to the table.

Dinner was served and Allegra was seated next to Antonia

Di Bona, a bony, sharp-faced woman in black crêpe. 'Stefano's kept you quiet,' she remarked, her voice light yet no less catty.

Allegra swallowed and glanced at Stefano across three feet of white damask. He was intent on a conversation with a colleague and she turned to smile coolly at Antonia. 'I'm just a friend.'

'Are you?' Antonia raised thin penciled-in eyebrows. 'Stefano doesn't have too many female friends.'

'No?' She felt a wave of relief flood through her although, coupled with it, was the needling awareness that Antonia knew something she didn't and was savouring the moment when she would tell her.

They ate their first course without much more conversation, but then Antonia turned to her again and there was malicious intent in her mocking smile.

'Have you known Stefano long, then?'

'Long enough,' Allegra replied carefully. Although there were probably few people who remembered or cared about her flight seven years ago, she knew they existed. How could they not, when their wedding had been fêted as the social event of the decade?

An event that had never happened. Allegra sought comfort in knowing that she'd called it all off early enough. No one would have gone to the church, no one would have known. She'd never asked her mother for details, how Stefano had responded when he'd been given her note, what he'd done or said.

She hadn't wanted to know, and she still didn't. The past, she reminded herself firmly, was forgotten.

'Long enough,' Antonia repeated. 'I wonder how long that is.' She leaned forward. 'You don't seem his type, you know. He prefers…' she paused, her hard, dark eyes sweeping Allegra's form with clear criticism '…more glamorous women. Do you go out with him very often?' She raised her eyebrows, smiling sweetly.

'No,' Allegra said coolly. Her face burned from Antonia's casual, cruel assessment, even though she told herself there was no reason to care. Antonia was simply one of those women who enjoyed taunting and tormenting other women. She wouldn't be happy until she was the last one standing and everyone else bore the scratches from her three-inch fake talons. 'I'm actually rather busy,' Allegra said, 'as is Stefano.' She knew she should explain that she was associated with Stefano only in a professional capacity, but she somehow couldn't form the words. Antonia probably wouldn't believe her, anyway.

Antonia gave a humourless little chuckle. 'Stefano is always busy. It's how he's become so rich.' She raked Allegra once with her cold eyes, then, bored, clearly dismissing her, added almost as an afterthought, 'It's also why his marriage failed.'

CHAPTER SIX

ALLEGRA FELT AS if she'd frozen, as if the very air around her had turned to ice and snow. She closed her eyes, then opened them. Across the table, she saw Stefano's gaze sweep over her, concern flickering across his features.

His marriage. He'd been married. Married, to someone else. Not to her, never to her. He'd loved someone else, had been with someone else, had said his vows to someone else.

Who?

She swallowed a sudden impulse to laugh, to laugh wildly and loudly until there was nothing left inside.

Why had he not told her? Where was his former wife?

Why was she so *hurt?*

A restive, rational part of her brain told her there was no reason to react this way, to *feel* this way. So Stefano had been married. True, he hadn't mentioned it, but why should he?

Professional.

Friends.

And yet nothing felt professional or friendly about their relationship right now. All Allegra could feel right now was the burning brand of Stefano's lips on hers, the hurt inside that she'd held back all these years, the girl inside who was still—still—crying out,

Do you love me?

She closed her eyes, willing the flood of feelings to recede.

She hadn't broken down for seven years and she wasn't about to break down now.

She wasn't about to break down ever.

She stiffened her shoulders, lifted her chin. Next to her, Antonia let out a raucous bird-like laugh as she chatted and flirted with the man on her other side.

Allegra heard the murmur of conversation around her, knew no one was paying attention to her, and tried to relax. She stared down at her uneaten dessert, a custard flan in a golden pool of syrup, and felt her stomach roil and rebel.

Relax.

So Stefano had been married. It didn't mean anything; it *wouldn't* mean anything to her.

And yet still…still. Still it mattered, still it meant something. She didn't want to think what, couldn't bear to analyse the feeling. Yet she already knew.

Hurt. It was hurt.

Allegra picked up her fork and took a bite of her dessert. It might as well have been cardboard for all she could taste; she was too preoccupied with this new awareness, this new hurt. Understanding and accepting it…and then dismissing it.

Why was she hurt? Why did she let him get under her skin, into her heart now? Still?

Always.

Allegra shook her head in instinctive, desperate denial. No. She wasn't that girl.

Do you love me?

She wasn't; she knew what he was like, had known for years. He'd bought her, had bought her like an object, a thing. And, worse, he'd treated her like one.

Not a treasure.

Never a treasure.

No matter what she'd wanted to convince herself of for a single evening's enjoyment.

She pushed her dessert away, took a sip of wine and felt

Stefano's eyes on her. He was chatting with a business col-league across the table, but his considering glance swept over her, and out of the corner of her eye Allegra saw his mouth tighten and knew he was aware that she was upset. He just didn't know why.

Dessert was cleared, coffee served, and Allegra forced herself to make small talk with the dowdy housewife on her left. Antonia had abandoned her completely, and Allegra could only be relieved. She didn't need any more well-placed catty remarks right now.

After the meal the guests circulated, chatting and laughing, while music from a string quartet played softly. Allegra moved through the elegant crowd, saw Stefano sweep the room with a hawk-eyed gaze. She wound her way through the throng and leaned against a cool marble pillar. She didn't know what she'd say to Stefano now, didn't even know what to think.

'Why are you hiding again?' Stefano had come behind her without her realizing it, and now she stiffened.

'I'm not hiding,' she retorted and he raised one eyebrow.

'You were avoiding me.'

She lifted her chin. 'Don't be so arrogant.'

'You're denying it?'

'I didn't feel like talking, Stefano, to you or anyone. I'm tired, and this isn't exactly my crowd.'

In answer he touched her chin with his fingertips, levelled her gaze to meet his own. 'What's wrong?' he asked quietly.

Something ached in Allegra. If only it were so simple, if only he really wanted to know. To understand.

If only he could make it better.

'Nothing,' she said through numb lips.

'You're upset.'

'Stop telling me what I am!' Allegra snapped, her voice rising enough so there was a lull in the conversation.

'You could mingle,' Stefano said mildly. 'Get to know people.'

Allegra kept her gaze averted. 'I don't feel like it.'

'I was hoping,' he continued in that aggravatingly calm voice, 'that we could enjoy ourselves this evening.'

She hunched one shoulder, her face averted. 'I'm tired, and I'm not really here to be your escort, am I, Stefano? Remember? I'm here to help Lucio. That's all.'

'You think I don't know that?' There was a savage edge to his voice that made Allegra's gaze slide nervously yet curiously to his. She was shocked to see his face, the hard lines and harsh angles of a man set in bitterness. In anger. 'You think I don't remind myself of that every day?' he demanded in a low voice.

Allegra shook her head, not daring to consider what he might mean. What he might want. 'Stefano…'

'Allegra, all I'm asking is that you act normally. Socialise. Chat. You used to be able to talk the hind leg off a donkey. I never got a word in edgewise. Have you changed so much?' He smiled then, and Allegra felt the revealing prickle of tears behind her lids.

She remembered those conversations, how she'd chattered and laughed about anything and everything—stupid, girlish, *childish* dreams—and Stefano had listened. He'd always listened.

'Stefano, don't,' she whispered.

He touched his thumb to her eyelid and it came away damp. 'Don't what?'

'Don't,' Allegra repeated helplessly. *Don't make me remember. Don't make me fall in love with you. You broke my heart once; I couldn't stand it again.*

The realization that it was in fact a possibility should have terrified her, but right now all Allegra felt was sad. She felt, perhaps for the first time, the sweet, piercing stab of regret.

She blinked, and Stefano's thumb came away wet again. 'Why are you crying?' he whispered and there was surprise and sorrow in his voice.

Allegra shook her head. 'I don't want to think about the past. I don't want to remember.'

'What about the good bits?' Stefano asked. 'There were some, weren't there?'

'Yes, but not enough.' She took a deep, steadying breath and then stepped away from Stefano's touch. 'Never enough.'

'No,' Stefano agreed, his voice odd, flat. 'Never enough.'

'Besides,' Allegra agreed, emboldened now that he wasn't touching her, 'you talk as if we had something real and deep and we didn't.' Another breath, more courage. 'Not, presumably, like you did with someone else.'

Stefano stilled, his expression deepening, darkening into a frown. 'What are you talking about?'

'I heard, Stefano,' Allegra said. She took another breath; her lungs hurt. Or maybe it was somewhere else, somewhere deeper that had absolutely no business being hurt. 'Antonia told me you were married.'

Even now Allegra expected him to deny it, to laugh even, or make some remark about how the closest he'd come to marriage was with her. Instead, a muscle flickered in his jaw and he gave a tiny shrug.

'It wasn't relevant.'

Allegra laughed; the sound carried on the air and people looked their way. 'It would have been nice to know.'

'Why, Allegra? Why would you need to know?' There was a fierce, blazing look in his eyes and on his face that had Allegra stepping back again.

'Just…just because,' she said, and her reasons and self-righteousness deserted her, leaving her with nothing but a few stammered excuses. 'It's the kind of thing I should—'

'Know?' Stefano finished. His voice was soft and dangerous. 'Do you ask all the adults you come in contact with about their marital history? The parents of the children you work with?' He smiled mockingly, his eyes hard and cold.

'You know it's not that simple,' Allegra snapped. 'Stop turning the tables on me, Stefano. You conveniently forget and remember the past—*our* past—however the mood strikes you! Well, allow me the same courtesy!' She realized, belatedly, that her voice had risen yet again. People were staring.

'This is not the place,' Stefano said between his teeth, 'for this discussion.'

She ignored him, shaking her head, the implications exploding through her mind. 'I don't even know if you're divorced. If you have children.'

'I'm widowed,' he bit out. 'I told you before, I have no children.' His hand clamped down on her elbow. 'Now we're going home.'

'Maybe I don't want to go home with *you!*' she said, jerking away from him, her voice rising to a shriek—a shriek people heard.

There was a moment of embarrassed silence, and then the conversation resumed at double speed and sound.

Allegra swallowed, felt colour stain her face and throat. She was making a scene. A big one.

And Stefano was angry about it—perhaps angrier than she'd ever seen him before.

'Are you quite finished?' he asked in a voice of arctic politeness.

Allegra couldn't look at him as she nodded. 'Yes. We can go,' she whispered.

'Perhaps we should stay,' Stefano told her in a deadly murmur, 'and brazen it out. But I'll have mercy…on both of us.' He took her elbow once more and guided her none too gently out of the ballroom.

She managed to hold her head high even though her face was aflame as Stefano escorted her from the room amid a hiss of speculative murmurs. They were both silent all the way to the car.

Vespas and taxis sped around them in a glitter of lights as they drove from the hotel to the quieter Parioli district.

Allegra sagged against the seat. Her behaviour, she knew, had been inexcusable. She should have waited to talk to Stefano back at his town house rather than force a full confrontation in the middle of an important business engagement.

She closed her eyes against the prickling of tears. He should have told her he'd been married.

No matter what he said now, what arguments he so reasonably gave her, he should have told her.

She should have known.

Why didn't she know? Allegra wondered. Why had she never heard? Surely, somewhere, somehow she should have known.

Perhaps she should have felt it.

And yet, a mocking voice asked her silently, why should you have known? Didn't you sever all ties when you left that night? She'd never seen her parents again; her father had died less than a year after, and her mother…

Her mother had got what she wanted. She lived her own life now in Milan, bankrolled by a steady stream of lovers.

As for anyone else who might have known of Stefano's marriage…who? Who were those people? The girls she'd known at convent school? The relatives who'd shunned her?

She'd made choices in life, instinctive choices that had kept her well away from Stefano and his circle. And, really, she hadn't wanted to know, had never asked anyone about Stefano, had avoided talking or even thinking about him. It was precisely this kind of information that she'd never wanted to hear.

Yet, in the end, none of it had worked, for here they were together, in this very car, the silence freezing and hostile, their knees still touching. And her heart was hurt, crying out once more.

The car pulled up to the town house and Allegra followed Stefano inside. She watched as he stalked into the drawing room and poured two fingers of Scotch into a glass and tossed it back.

He stood in front of the fireplace, one hand braced against the marble mantle. Outside, a car drove past and washed the room in sickly yellow light. Allegra closed the double doors, drew the curtains and turned on a lamp. All tasks to keep her from the reckoning she knew would come. What she knew she had to say.

'I'm sorry.'

'For what?' Stefano asked, a trace of sarcasm sharpening his tone. 'For seeing me again? For agreeing to help Lucio? Or perhaps for walking out on me in the first place?'

There was such savagery in his voice that Allegra could only push it away, refuse to consider the implications of his words, the turn in his tone.

'No,' she said quickly, 'for my behaviour tonight. I was shocked that you were married and I...I overreacted at the party.'

'Yes, you did.'

Her fingers nervously pleated the silk of her gown. 'Why didn't you tell me?'

'Why should I have?'

'Because...' She tried to think of a reason, a safe one. 'Because I deserve to know,' she finally said. 'We've acknowledged the past and forgotten about it, but...'

'But it's still there.'

'Yes.' Allegra bit her lip. 'I never heard that you'd married.'

'Did you ever ask?'

'No, of course not. Why would I...?' She trailed off, not wanting to follow that line of thought and its inevitable conclusions.

'You wouldn't have heard,' Stefano said after a moment, his voice resigned, 'because it was kept quiet. By me.'

'Why?' she whispered.

He turned around and Allegra was surprised and alarmed by the weariness etched into his features. 'Because I regretted it almost as soon as the ceremony was over.'

He ran a hand through his hair before sinking into a cream silk armchair. 'If you want the facts, Allegra, I'll give them to you. I suppose I should have considered that someone might mention my marriage to you tonight, but I didn't want to deal with it. Not yet, anyway. So I just pushed it away and didn't think about it.' A smile flickered and died, and his eyes were shrewd. 'A habit I believe we share.'

Allegra looked down. The man in front of her was one she

wasn't used to. Here was Stefano being candid, open. Vulnerable. He sat sprawled in a chair, his tie loosened and the top two buttons of his shirt undone, his whisky tumbler still held loosely in one hand.

'So what are the facts?' she asked in a low voice.

'I was married to Gabriella Capoleti for six years.'

'Six years!' It came out in a shattered, shocked gasp. Six *years*. 'When did you marry her?'

'Three months after you left me,' Stefano said flatly.

Left me. Not Italy, not the wedding, no innocent, innocuous phrases. *Left me.* Because that was what she'd really done.

Allegra felt dizzy, and she steadied herself by placing one hand on the back of a chair. 'Why?' she whispered. 'Why so soon?'

Stefano shrugged, gave the ghost of a smile. 'My first marriage didn't happen, so I planned another.'

'That simple,' Allegra whispered.

Stefano smiled, although his eyes were hard. 'Yes.'

She swallowed. Why did this hurt? This was old ground they were covering. She'd raked it over in her own mind years ago, had laid it to rest. Yet now it felt fresh, raw, achingly painful.

It hurt.

'I meant to marry you for your name, Allegra, remember? The Avesti name.' He laughed dryly, without humour. 'Not that the Avesti name has any standing these days.'

'Don't—'

'No, you don't like to face that, do you?' Stefano said, his voice as sharp and cutting as a blade. 'You don't like to face the facts. Well, neither do I. I try not to think of my marriage. Ever.'

'Why not?' Her throat felt like sandpaper; her eyes were dry and gritty. 'Did you love her?'

'Does it matter?' Stefano asked in a soft hiss. 'To you?'

Yes. 'No.' Allegra drew herself up. 'No, of course not. I just wondered.'

Stefano was silent; so was she. Waiting. Wondering. Outside she heard the muted blare of a car horn, the trill of a woman's laughter.

'I married Gabriella for the Capoleti name, just as I was going to marry you for yours,' Stefano finally said. His voice was as flat as if he were reciting a list of dry, dusty facts. 'I needed someone from an old, established family.'

'Why did you need a name so much?' Allegra asked, wondering even now why she hadn't asked this, thought this before. She'd just shut it all out.

His lips curved in a smile and his eyes glittered like topaz. 'Because I don't have one myself, of course. I have money. That's all.' She heard a bleak note in his voice that she didn't completely understand.

'And so Gabriella accepted this arrangement?' Her voice sharpened as she added, 'Or did you deceive her as well?'

Stefano gazed at her for a moment, his expression assessing. Knowing. 'As I deceived you?' he finished softly. 'How you cling to that, Allegra. How you need to believe it.'

'Of course I believe it,' Allegra snapped. 'I heard it from my father's mouth, from your own! Our marriage was nothing more than a business deal, brokered between the two of you.' Rage and self-righteousness made her stand tall, straight. Proud. 'How much was I worth in the end, Stefano? How much did you pay for me?'

Stefano laughed softly. 'Didn't you realize? Nothing, Allegra. I paid nothing for you.' She blinked; he smiled. 'But I *would* have paid a million euros for you, if you'd shown up that day. A million euros your father had already gambled away. That was why he killed himself, you know. He was in debt— far more than a million euros in debt. And, when you didn't marry me, he got nothing.'

Allegra closed her eyes, wished she could close her mind against what Stefano was saying.

'More facts,' Stefano said softly, 'that you've never wanted to face.'

He was right, she knew. She'd never wanted to face the fallout of her flight, had never wanted to examine too closely why her father had killed himself, why her mother had run.

'It's not my fault,' she whispered, and her voice cracked.

'Does it really matter?' Stefano returned.

She shook her head, shut herself off from those memories, those emotions. 'What of Gabriella, then? Tell me about your marriage.'

'Gabriella was thirty years old then—two years older than me at the time. Desperate, to be blunt. She agreed to the marriage, to the *arrangement,* and it all happened rather quickly.'

'So it would seem.' Allegra sank into a chair. She felt sick. She'd always known that Stefano had his reasons for marrying her... Hadn't her mother said, *Our social connections, his money?* Yet here was the proof, right in front of her that he'd never loved her, had never cared in the least. He was giving it to her.

He was telling her, and he didn't even sound sorry. Just resigned.

'Why did you keep it quiet,' she finally asked, 'if you wanted her name? Shouldn't you have...let people know?' Her voice wobbled with uncertainty and Stefano raised his eyebrows.

'Cash in on my investment? In theory, yes. But I realized after I married Gabriella that I didn't want her damned name. I didn't want her, and she didn't want me.' He laughed dryly, but Allegra heard something else in that sound, something sad and broken. 'And, in the end, I realized I didn't want to build my business on someone else's shoulders. I'd got as far as I had by myself, or nearly, and I'd continue the same way.' He gave the ghost of a smile.

Allegra gave a little jerk of assent, her eyes sliding from Stefano and the bitterness and cynicism radiating from him in icy, intangible waves.

'So what happened?' she finally whispered. 'She...she died?'

'Yes.' Stefano raised his eyes to meet her startled gaze. 'But six weeks after the wedding Gabriella left me. I don't blame her. I was miserable company and a poor husband.' He leaned his head back against the chair. 'She went to live in Florence, in a flat I provided for her. We agreed to live completely separate lives. When she died in a car accident six months ago, I hadn't seen her for nearly five years.'

'But…but that's horrible,' Allegra whispered.

'Yes,' Stefano agreed bleakly, 'it is.'

'What…what did you do that made her so miserable? To leave you?'

He raised one eyebrow, his smile darkly sardonic. 'My fault, is it?'

'You admitted it was!'

Stefano was silent for a long time, his head back, his eyes closed. Allegra wondered if he'd actually fallen asleep.

Then he spoke, his eyes still closed. 'I realized I wanted something else from marriage. Something more. And so did Gabriella. Unfortunately, we couldn't give it to each other.'

'What was it?' Allegra asked in a whisper.

Slowly Stefano raised his head, opened his eyes. Allegra felt transfixed by his sleepy gaze, gold glinting in his irises. 'What do you think it was, Allegra?'

'I…' She licked her lips. She didn't know. What more did Stefano want from a marriage? He'd got the social connections, he had the money. What more was there to be gained? 'I…I don't know.'

'I wonder,' Stefano mused, turning his tumbler around and around between his palms, 'why you were so startled by the fact of my marriage. It almost seemed as if you were *hurt*.'

Allegra jerked back. 'Of course I was startled! It's rather a large fact to keep secret—'

'But you've kept secrets, Allegra,' Stefano interjected softly, 'haven't you? I haven't been celibate for the last seven years. Neither, I believe, have you.'

Allegra felt as if she'd been nailed to the chair. The last thing she'd expected now was for him to turn the spotlight on *her*.

'What does that matter?' she finally asked, trying to keep her voice cool. Logical.

'Exactly. What does that matter? If I choose to ignore your past, then you should ignore mine, don't you think? Because it doesn't matter, since you're merely here in a professional capacity.' His eyes glittered and he leaned forward. 'Does it?'

'No,' Allegra said, her voice sounding hollow to her own ears, 'it doesn't.'

She felt the truth of what he was saying, what he was implying, like a series of electric shocks to her heart. Because it did matter. It did hurt.

And the only reason it could was because Stefano still mattered. To her.

'How many lovers have you had, Allegra?' Stefano asked softly.

Allegra felt as if an icy finger had trailed along her spine, drifted across her cheek. She didn't like the look in Stefano's eyes, the intent, the anger. 'Stefano,' she said, her face pale, her voice thready, 'it doesn't matter. I never married you, I was free. I'm not yours to command, to possess. It doesn't matter how many lovers I've had.' Her voice shook. 'You shouldn't even ask.'

'But it does matter,' Stefano replied, his voice still so soft, so dangerous. 'It matters to me.'

'Why?' She was trembling—actually trembling—under the onslaught of his blazing gaze.

He didn't answer, just smiled. 'Who was the man who touched you first?' he asked softly. 'Who touched you where I should have touched you?'

Allegra closed her eyes. Images danced in the darkness of her closed lids; imaginary images that had never taken place, memories of Stefano and her that had never been made.

'Don't, Stefano,' she whispered. 'You don't want to do this.'

'No, I don't,' Stefano agreed, his voice pleasant, a parody. 'I know I don't, and I shouldn't. But I'm going to do it anyway. Who was he? When did you have your first lover?'

Her eyes were still closed, but she heard—felt—him move. He closed the small space between them and she knew he was standing before her. She heard him drop down to kneel in front of her, felt his hands on her knees. She tensed, he waited.

The moment was endless. They were so close, yet a yawning chasm had opened between them, a chasm caused by memories they'd both claimed didn't matter. Memories they'd said they'd forgotten.

Allegra felt them tumble through her mind; she saw Stefano smile, she remembered the light touch of his carefully chaste kiss, she even felt the exploding joy within her at being loved.

She'd thought she'd been loved.

But, of course, she hadn't. Not then, and certainly not now.

She gave a little gasp as she felt his fingers skim her knees, testing, teasing. Touching.

And his touch, as it had all those years ago, caused sensation to explode in her stomach, to spiral upwards from her heart. Her *heart*.

'Stefano…' she whispered, and stopped, because she didn't know what she was saying. She didn't even know what she was wanting.

She knew that if they continued down this path it would be dangerous. Deadly. How could they recover, continue the polite parody of their relationship, when *this* had happened?

This. Desire. Regret. Wonder.

Slowly, Stefano slid his hand along the tender, untouched skin of her thigh. Allegra shuddered lightly, but kept her eyes closed. She didn't want to open them, didn't want to see the expression on Stefano's face. She was afraid of what it would be, what he was feeling.

What *she* was feeling.

'Did he touch you here?' he whispered. His hand slipped along her thigh, his fingers drifting higher, closer. Allegra felt her legs part, leaving her passive to his calculated caress.

She shook her head, not even sure what she was denying, admitting. Wanting him to stop, yet also wanting him to continue. Treacherously, terribly, wanting him to continue, even now.

'What about here?' Stefano whispered. His fingers played with the elastic of her underwear, his thumb skimming over her most sensitive flesh. 'Did you enjoy it? Did you...?' His finger slipped beneath her underwear. 'Did you think of me?'

She gasped aloud, whether in pleasure or shame even she didn't know. Her eyes were still closed, clenched shut. She gave a little shake of her head.

She opened her eyes, saw his blaze into hers with feeling. Anger. *Hatred.*

Shock reverberated through her at the savage expression on his face, his soul reflected so openly, so terribly, if only for a moment.

'What is this?' she choked out. 'Some kind of *revenge?*'

Stefano's eyes burned into hers for one fiery second before he cursed under his breath and jerked back. Allegra watched him stalk across the room, his back to her, heard the clink of glass as he poured himself another whisky.

She sagged against the chair, limp, lifeless. He was treating her like a possession, she thought. Just as she'd feared he would all those years ago, just as she'd always known. A possession. *His.* His to punish.

He was *punishing* her, she knew with a cold fury quite apart from the desire he'd sent spiralling through her.

Punishing her, for having had a lover when he'd been married. The realization of such a disgusting double standard cleared her head, gave her strength.

'It was a doctor at the hospital where I was training,' she said, and her voice was clipped and cold. Stefano stilled but did not turn around. 'David Stirling. We were lovers for two months, until I realized he was just about as controlling and possessive as you are. And,' she added, her voice shaking, 'we didn't sleep together until last year. So I waited six years to give myself to someone else, Stefano. You waited three months.'

He still didn't turn around, and she wanted to hurt him, wound him, as he'd wounded her. Yet she knew she couldn't, because he didn't care.

And she did. Damn it, she did.

'And you're right, it doesn't matter. It doesn't matter because you don't care about me, Stefano. You never did. You never loved me. The only thing that was hurt when I left was your wretched pride. You showed it tonight—someone else got to play with your toy! That's all I am, have ever been, to you. And,' she continued, trembling with emotion, with the river of suppressed feeling coursing through her in a terrible, unrelenting stream, 'even if you had loved me, I didn't want the kind of love you were prepared to give—a kind that didn't involve honesty or joy or anything that really matters.'

Protection. Provision. *What more is there?*

He still didn't turn around, didn't acknowledge her in any way but the stiffness of his shoulders.

Allegra felt a blinding anger driving through to a needlepoint of pain, anger and pain that fuelled her words. 'The kind of love you offer, Stefano, isn't love. It's nothing! It's *worthless.*'

Stefano jerked, though he didn't turn around. For a triumphant second Allegra actually thought she'd got to him. Hurt him. Yet even as she felt a blaze of victory, she realized it didn't feel the way she wanted it to—deep and satisfying, a direct hit.

She felt low, cheapened somehow by her own actions as well as Stefano's.

She took a breath, trying to calm herself. 'Coming here was obviously a mistake but it's also a business arrangement.' She laughed, a sharp, brittle sound. 'Just like our marriage was meant to be! Funny, how it all comes round. I'll stay, Stefano, for Lucio's sake. I want to help him. But when I have, and the next few months, or however long it takes, are over, I'll thank God that I never have to see you again. A welcome thought for you as well, I'm sure.'

Trembling, still aching to hit him, hurt him, make him at least turn around and acknowledge her, Allegra left the room. She slammed the door on the way out.

Stefano knew he shouldn't have a third whisky but he felt like it. He wasn't a man who normally drank, but now he needed the fiery relief burning all the way to his gut.

Rage and remorse coursed through him in an unrelenting river of emotion. Emotion he didn't want to acknowledge, much less feel.

Damn it. Why had he talked to her, treated her like that?

Allegra. The woman who was going to help Lucio. The woman meant to be his wife. He hadn't forgotten. He could never forget the moment when he'd realized, when he'd known that she'd left. And she hadn't bothered to say goodbye, to explain.

Nothing but a note.

That moment was burned into his memory, into his very soul. It felt as much a part of him as his family, his job, his every ambition or fear. He'd carried it around with him for seven years; he wasn't about to let it go.

Yet, for Lucio's sake, he had to. He had to try.

When he'd decided to seek Allegra out, to hire her, he'd convinced himself that the past didn't matter. *She* didn't matter.

There was no reason to care what she'd done, who she'd been with, who she'd loved. He'd been married, of all things; he could hardly accuse her for taking a lover. She was twenty-six years old and she had every right to find romance, love, *sex*, with someone else.

Someone other than him.

Yet the reality of it had been much harder to bear than the mere possibility.

It wasn't the idea of another man touching her that wounded, Stefano realized with profound bitterness, although that certainly stung. It was the fact that Allegra had chosen—had preferred—

someone else. She'd walked away from him to seek solace in another's arms, and nothing—*nothing*—could change that.

Even worse, perhaps, was the cold, hard knowledge that he'd done the same thing. And failed.

The only solace he'd found was in knowing he'd made a mistake, and doing his best to rectify it. Giving Gabriella her life, her freedom back had been a relief for both of them.

Stefano dragged in a long, laborious breath and set his tumbler down. He walked slowly from the room, up the stairs to Allegra's bedroom.

He didn't try the knob; he had a feeling it would be locked and he didn't want to find out. He placed his palm flat on the door, leaned his forehead against the smooth wood. All was silent, but he spoke anyway.

'Allegra.'

He thought he heard a tiny sniff, a little gasp. He continued. 'I'm sorry. I shouldn't have said or done what I did downstairs. It was wrong of me. I...' He paused, his throat closing against the clamour of things he felt but didn't know how to say. 'Goodnight,' he finally managed, and walked slowly down the corridor to his own empty bedroom.

CHAPTER SEVEN

THE NEXT MORNING the town house was silent as Allegra made her way downstairs, but after a few seconds she heard the quiet clink of china from the dining room and saw Stefano in the mahogany-panelled room, drinking a cappuccino, his head bent over the newspaper.

She watched him silently for a moment, the hard plane of his cheek and jaw, the soft sweep of his hair, the way he absently ran his long-fingered hand through it before turning a page.

Looking longer she saw lines of strain on either side of his mouth, shadows of fatigue under his eyes.

What had kept him up last night? she wondered. His own behaviour, or hers? The past or the future?

It was wrong of me.

She'd heard him through her door, as she huddled on her bed. She'd heard the regret in his voice, but it barely made a dent in her hardened heart.

He'd treated her like an object. A possession. He'd revealed himself in that one cold, calculated caress—what he thought of her, what he couldn't forget.

And even though the light touch of his fingers had made her tremble, had made her want, she wouldn't let it weaken her will.

She was not Stefano's possession. She would not let him treat her as one. *Ever.*

And, Allegra resolved as she stood in the doorway of the

dining room, she would tell Stefano so. Now, not with whispered words of regret through a closed door, but face to face, eye to eye.

'Stefano.'

His head jerked up, his eyes wary, hooded before he smiled. '*Buon giorno.*'

'*Buon giorno.*' She sat at the table and picked up a *cornetti,* taking a knife and buttering it with fingers that only trembled a tiny bit. 'We need to talk.'

He folded his paper and placed it on the table, a look of polite expectancy on his face. 'Of course. What is it?'

She shook her head slowly. Was he going to pretend that last night hadn't happened? That the truth, painful and broken as it was, hadn't been revealed?

'When we both agreed to this business arrangement,' she began, keeping her voice firm and purposeful, 'you told me that we were different people. That the past didn't matter.'

'Yes,' Stefano confirmed, a touch of coolness in his voice. He took a sip of his coffee and Anna bustled in from the kitchen with a cappuccino for Allegra.

'*Grazie,*' she murmured, her gaze still fastened on Stefano's. 'But that wasn't true, was it, Stefano?' she asked softly when Anna had left. 'The past does matter, and perhaps we haven't changed as much as we think we have. As much as we want to have changed. And I won't allow the past to affect the present or the future. Not my future, not yours, and certainly not Lucio's.'

'I wouldn't expect it to,' Stefano drawled. He sounded bored.

'You may have hired me,' Allegra continued, her voice still thankfully firm, 'but I'm not your possession. I won't be treated like one—'

'Allegra, I apologised for my behaviour last night,' Stefano cut her off coldly. 'I was angry with what had happened, not seven years before, but a few hours ago. You behaved in a childish way at the dinner, and I responded by behaving in a childish manner here. Again, I'm sorry.' He gave her a tight, perfunctory smile that sent fury coursing through her in a cleansing stream.

'I'd accept that,' she said, 'if you'd called me names or thrown a tantrum. *Childish* behaviour. But that wasn't it, was it, Stefano? It was something more.' She paused, took a breath. Stefano waited, one eyebrow raised in scathing scepticism. 'The truth is,' Allegra continued, 'you can't forget the past, you can't pretend it doesn't affect the present and any future. I believed we could because I wanted to believe it, because it was easier. But in the end ignoring it will only make it more difficult, for you, for me, and for Lucio—'

'That's quite an interesting load of psychobabble,' Stefano cut her off. 'Did you learn it on your art therapy course?'

'No, I learned it through dealing with you,' Allegra snapped. 'The way you treated me—' She stopped, pressed her lips together and refused to think about how his fingers had sought her, punished her, thrilled her. And then, worst and most hurtful of all: the blazing look of contempt, *cruelty* in his eyes. 'But last night proved to me that you're the same man you were seven years ago, treating me the same way.' The words rang with contempt and condemnation, but Stefano didn't react. He merely stilled, his face blank, his eyes hard. Silence. Yet again the only response to her words, her plea for understanding, was silence.

She heard the ticking of the clock, the clink of china as Stefano carefully, slowly stirred his coffee. 'Think what you like,' he finally said. He looked up, smiled in a way that was utterly chilling to Allegra. It was the smile, she thought numbly, of a person who didn't care at all. And, she realized, even now she wanted him to care.

'It doesn't really matter. I apologised for my behaviour, and it won't happen again. As you said,' Stefano continued in a voice of determined pleasantness, 'you're here to help Lucio. We don't need to deal with each other at all.'

'It's not that simple—'

'It will be,' Stefano said, and there was hard finality to his words, his face. 'It will be.'

Allegra tried once more. 'Unless we deal with it, with our feelings—'

Stefano laughed. Allegra didn't like the sound. 'But I don't have *feelings* for you, Allegra, remember? I bought you. I treated you like a possession. I *thought* of you as a possession...you told me so yourself. Why should I have feelings for an object?'

Allegra opened her mouth, closed it, and then opened it again. 'But...'

'So if I didn't have feelings for you then,' he continued, cutting across her useless, incoherent denial, his voice horribly soft, 'why should I now?'

But he wasn't finished. His eyes glittered as he leaned forward, his voice thrumming with power and knowledge. 'You want to talk about *feelings,* Allegra?' he challenged. 'What about yours?'

Allegra drew back. 'What about mine?'

'You think I'm the only one who doesn't like to talk about the past? What about you? What about the fact that you haven't seen your mother or your father since that night you ran away?'

'My father's dead,' Allegra said. 'Stefano, this has nothing—'

'To do with it? Perhaps it does. You don't want to face what you've done. Well, neither do I.' His voice was quiet and controlled, yet Allegra felt as if he were shouting. She felt as if he were shouting at her. 'Why did you cut off all contact with your family? You stayed at your father's funeral for less than an hour. I know. I was there.'

Her mouth opened, yet no words came out. He gave her a faint feral smile, yet she saw a bleakness in his eyes, a bleakness Allegra felt herself.

'I watched you from afar. You never saw me.'

'Why did you come?'

'I knew your father too, Allegra. I shared in the guilt for his death. He was a foolish man, even an immoral one, but no one deserves to suffer such despair.'

Allegra held up one hand as if to ward off his words, as if they were blows. 'Don't—'

'It hurts, doesn't it?' Stefano said softly. 'To remember.'

'*Stefano*—'

'You cut yourself off from everything and everyone you'd ever known, Allegra,' Stefano said, every word a condemnation. 'Even yourself.'

'You don't know—'

'Because you couldn't face it. You don't want to face it. So don't ask me to face anything, when you've been running from the past for seven years, and you *still* haven't stopped.'

'This is not about me!' Allegra shrieked. Her voice felt as if it had been ripped from her lungs and her chest, heaving with emotion, hurt. 'This is not about me,' she said again, and this time her voice cracked.

'No? None of it's about you?' Stefano rose from the table, his face harsh, his voice utterly merciless. 'What about your father, Allegra? Did he have nothing to do with you? I know he was crushed by your betrayal. I know it was one of the reasons he killed himself.'

'No.' She wouldn't think of it. She wouldn't allow him to make her think of it. Like a steel trap, the lid of the box Stefano had ripped open snapped shut. Allegra felt herself go numb— numb and cold, blessedly blank. She rose from the table too, curling her hands around the back of her chair to steady herself. 'You don't know what you're talking about,' she said in a flat, cold voice quite unlike her own.

Stefano laughed shortly. 'I think I know all too well. But it's better this way, isn't it? For both of us.' He turned away. 'We leave for Abruzzo within the hour.'

'Fine.' Allegra nodded, still numb. It was so much easier not to feel. Not to feel anything.

Yet, as he left, she found her legs going weak and it all came rushing back, a tide of emotion she couldn't deal with. Wouldn't deal with. Allegra sank into her chair, dropped her head in her hands.

Whatever either of them tried to believe, the past was not forgotten. It was alive and well and vibrating between them with a thousand torturous memories.

The sun was high and bright in the sky when they pulled away from the narrow street and into the clogged city traffic. Stefano was dressed casually in jeans and a crisp white shirt, the sleeves rolled back against his forearms.

'I think you'll like Abruzzo,' he said when they'd cleared the traffic and the road stretched endlessly ahead of them, winding through dusty brown hills and fields of sunflowers ready for harvest. He spoke in a pleasant, impersonal tone that Allegra knew she should be thankful for but instead it grated on her nerves, made her hands clench in her lap. 'It's very relaxing there, very quiet. A good place for you to work with Lucio.'

'I look forward to it,' she said tersely, her face averted.

'Good.'

They'd silently agreed on a tense truce, and Allegra wondered how long it would last. For Lucio's sake, she couldn't be distracted by Stefano when she worked with him. She knew that, saw it as her first consideration, and she knew Stefano did as well.

At least on that point—the only point, it seemed—they were in agreement.

They both lapsed into silence and drove that way for an hour as the plains and fields around Rome turned hilly, and then mountainous. In the distance Allegra glimpsed rolling fields of saffron, the small purple flowers with their distinctive red-gold stigma stretching to the craggy, snow-topped peak of Gran Sasso.

Stefano turned off the motorway and they drove on a small winding road through several hill towns, huddled against the unforgiving landscape as if they had but a desperate, precarious hold on this earth.

Allegra glimpsed an old woman, dressed from head to toe in black, leading a bony cow along the road. She grinned toothlessly at them, her eyes lost in wrinkles, and Stefano raised one hand in greeting as the car passed by.

There could be no mistaking that this region of Abruzzo was impoverished. Although she'd seen signs on the motorway for ski resorts, spas and luxury hotels, here the hill towns showed no signs of such wealth. The streets were narrow and near empty, the few houses and shops sporting peeling paint and crooked shutters. It was as if time had simply passed by these places, Allegra thought, and no one living there had even noticed.

They drove through another town and out into the countryside again, the rolling, rocky hills leading to mountains, a few falling down farmhouses huddled against the hillside, half a dozen sheep grazing on the desolate landscape.

'What made you buy a farmhouse out here?' Allegra asked, breaking an hour long silence.

Stefano's fingers flexed on the wheel. 'I told you, it's my home.'

'You mean you grew up here? I always thought you were from Rome.'

'Near Rome,' Stefano corrected, his eyes on the twisting road. 'We're less than a hundred kilometres from Rome, believe it or not.'

Allegra couldn't believe it. The harsh beauty of this landscape was so different from the ostentatious wealth and glamour of the Eternal City.

She also couldn't imagine that Stefano came from this place. She'd always assumed he was urban, urbane, born to wealth and luxury if not aristocratic pedigree and privilege.

'Your family had a villa here?' she asked cautiously and he gave a short laugh.

'You could say that.'

He swung sharply on to an even narrower road, little more than dirt and pebbles, and they drove in silence for a few minutes more before coming to a sleepy village with only a handful of shops and houses. A few old men sat outside a café, playing chess and drinking coffee, and they looked up as Stefano drove through. They squinted at the car before cheers erupted from the café crowd and Stefano slowed the car to a stop.

'Just a moment,' he said, and Allegra watched in bemusement as he climbed out of the car and approached the men. They were impoverished old farmers, their remaining teeth tobacco-stained, greasy caps crammed on their heads.

Allegra watched as the men embraced Stefano in turn, kissed his cheeks and clapped him on the back. She looked on with growing surprise and wonder as Stefano kissed them back, held them by the shoulders and greeted them with the respect and love of a beloved son.

They talked for a few moments, loudly and with much excitement and agitation, and then Stefano turned to her, his expression tense and still, and beckoned for her to come out of the car.

Slowly Allegra did so. She was not a snob, and she'd certainly been among the lowest of society's offerings in her seven years in London.

Yet, she realized, she'd thought Stefano was a snob. After all, he'd wanted to marry her for her social connections. He'd married someone else for them.

He put paid to that assumption by the way he laughed and smiled with these men, old and incredibly poor. He looked upon them as if they were his family, Allegra thought. As if he loved them.

'*Por* Lucio,' Stefano said. 'She is going to help him.'

Allegra heard a chorus of grateful and delighted cries. *Fantastico! Fantastico! Grazie, grazie, magnifico!* And then she was embraced as he'd been, her face cradled by weathered hands as kisses were bestowed on each cheek, and she heard the men murmuring '*Grazie, grazie*' in a heartfelt chorus of thankfulness.

Tears stung her eyes at their easy affection, their unsullied joy. She smiled back, found herself laughing, returning the warm embraces even though she knew not one person's name.

She felt rather than saw Stefano watching her, felt both his tension and approval. The men wouldn't let them go back in the car until they'd drunk a toast, the conversation continuing with a round of questions.

Would she stay long? Did she know Lucio—such a wonderful child? And Enzo—a man with such wisdom, such kindness! It was a tragedy, such a tragedy…

Allegra listened, nodding with deepening sympathy for this close community and the sorrow that had ripped it apart.

And yet Enzo's death *hadn't* ripped it beyond repair, she realized. If anything, it had made these men, this community, stronger. Closer. They clearly all cared deeply about Lucio, about Bianca…about Stefano.

She thought of her own family, the sorrow and betrayal which had left it in shreds. She thought of Stefano's words only this morning, *You haven't seen your mother or your father since that night you ran away,* and then her mind slid gratefully away.

She turned her thoughts back to Stefano, saw him smiling and laughing good-naturedly, his arm around the shoulders of one of the men who looked at him with the love of a father shining in his eyes.

Finally Stefano made his excuses and they returned to the car. People crowded around the windows, women in black and ragged children who laughed and slapped the windows in excitement.

Stefano honked the horn a few times to many more delighted cries, and then they drove off.

They drove in silence for a few minutes. Allegra's mind whirled with questions. She hadn't expected Stefano to act like that, to have such a genuine camaraderie with a bunch of poor farmers.

She glanced at him, saw his eyes on the road, and ventured cautiously, 'Those men loved you.'

'They are fathers to me,' Stefano said. He spoke in a voice that brooked no questions, no comments. Allegra nodded even though her mind seethed with both.

She was ashamed to realize she knew nothing about Stefano's family. Where was his own father, mother? Did he have brothers or sisters? What kind of childhood, what kind of *life,* had he had?

She didn't know.

And, she realized with a rush of surprise, she wished she did. She wished she'd asked when she'd had the chance.

It was too late for that, she thought. Too late for both of them. The only relationship that could exist between them was one of distant professionalism. It was what she'd wanted all along, what she'd insisted on, yet now it made her sad.

Stupid. How could she be wanting something from Stefano now—*now*—when it was so clear that he wanted to give her nothing? Nothing she needed, anyway.

Finally Stefano turned into a long dirt drive, twisted oak trees shading the lane. Allegra glimpsed a farmhouse on one side of the road, a crude place with its roof caving in. She wondered why Stefano left such an eyesore on his property before her sights and senses were taken with the villa in front of them.

It was not ostentatious, Allegra saw at once, but it possessed every comfort. Begonias and geraniums spilled from hanging baskets and terracotta urns that lined the flagstone path up to the front door.

A young woman with luxuriant dark hair caught up in a bun opened the door and called a welcome. A little boy with the same dark, glossy hair stood next to her, keeping himself close to his mother yet also strangely, inexorably apart.

'My housekeeper, Bianca,' Stefano said quietly, 'and that is Lucio.'

Allegra nodded, saw the boy stare into an unknown—and safe—middle distance. They climbed out of the car and she noticed that the air was sharp and cool, scented with pine and cedar.

'Bianca.' Stefano greeted her warmly and Allegra was ashamed to feel a piercing little stab of jealousy. 'Hello, Lucio.' He ruffled the boy's dark hair, but Lucio didn't look at him, didn't say a word.

Stefano introduced her to Bianca, who shook her hand and smiled with hopeful gratitude. Allegra crouched down so she was eye-level with Lucio. His eyes didn't meet hers, but still she smiled as if he were looking at her.

'Hello, Lucio,' she said quietly. 'I'm happy to meet you.'

Lucio didn't look at her, didn't acknowledge her at all. It was as if she hadn't spoken, or even as if she wasn't even there.

Allegra hadn't expected him to speak or even look at her, yet his utter indifference betrayed by not even one flicker of understanding was discouraging. Still she remained there, crouched down, for several long moments. She knew Lucio had to be aware of her on some level, and that would have to be enough. For now.

She stood up and Bianca ushered them into the house.

Allegra glanced around, surprised again. Stefano's town house in Rome had been the epitome of tasteful, if impersonal, luxury. This house had no obvious antiques or original paintings, no clear signs of wealth or status.

Yet it was a home—comfortable and well cared for. Well loved. Bianca led them into the kitchen rather than the lounge, and Allegra could see that this was the heart of the house. A wide oak table occupied one side of the room, the gleaming kitchen appliances the other. In the middle an alcove had been made, three sides were windows to the world.

Allegra stepped into the alcove and gasped, for it had been built directly on to a rocky outcrop and she felt as if she were standing on a mountain top. She felt as if she could fly.

'Careful, don't fall,' Stefano murmured from behind her. His hand lightly touched her waist.

'I feel like I could topple right off,' Allegra admitted with a little laugh. 'But it's wonderful.'

'I'm glad you like it.'

She glanced at him. 'Did you build this house yourself?'

'I helped design it.'

Bianca bustled over to them. 'You must be hungry from your journey. Lunch, *signor?* And *signorina?* You can eat here or in the dining room.'

'Here,' Allegra said with decision. She gazed out at the hills stretching emptily, endlessly to the magnificent peaks of the Apennines and felt a small, surprising *frisson* of happiness.

She liked it here, she realized. She liked the solitude, the possibility of serenity. She liked the idea that this house was a glimpse into Stefano's life, the man he was now...and perhaps had been all along. A man different from the one she thought she'd known.

Good things could happen here, she told herself. Good things for Lucio, and perhaps even good things for herself. She just didn't know what those things might be. She couldn't—wouldn't—even begin to guess.

Bianca served lunch and Allegra tucked in to spaghetti alla chitarra—square strands of pasta with a spicy tomato sauce and the local pecorino cheese.

Despite both her and Stefano's urging, Bianca refused to eat with them, and Lucio still didn't say a word or even look at them. Allegra told Bianca it would take a few days for Lucio to accept her presence, and until then the real work—the art therapy—could not begin. Bianca nodded, although disappointment flashed briefly in her dark eyes.

No matter what anyone said or didn't say, Allegra knew, everyone secretly wanted a miracle.

Did she?

The thought surprised her with its unexpectedness as well as its force. Bianca and her son had left for their own rooms in the back of the house, and she and Stefano were alone.

She glanced at him now, preoccupied and yet more relaxed than he'd been in either London or Rome.

Was she expecting a miracle with Stefano? Why, when she shouldn't expect anything?

He didn't love her; he never had. And while she'd once loved him with all the passion and feeling in her childish heart, she didn't love him now. He'd treated her terribly last night; she should hate him.

As he, perhaps, hated her.

And yet she still found herself wondering about the man he really was...the man who had designed this amazing villa, who had embraced those poor farmers like fathers and friends. The man who cared deeply about his housekeeper's son, a boy other wealthy, prominent businessmen wouldn't even be aware existed.

Who was that man? she wondered. And why had she never bothered to find out? Seven years ago, it had been enough that Stefano loved her, or at least seemed to. His attention, his little gifts, even his smile had been enough.

Now, Allegra realized, she wanted more. She wanted intimacy, understanding. She wanted to see him turn to her with laughter and warmth instead of distance and wary regard. She wanted him to touch her with desire that was not tarnished by anger, by memory.

She wanted *more*.

More, and yet there could be nothing between them, for Lucio's sake, and certainly for their own. The past was forgotten and there was no future.

Allegra toyed with her pasta. Stefano's gaze had settled on the distant hills and he seemed lost in his thoughts.

'This is your home,' she stated after a moment, and Stefano smiled faintly.

'Yes, I said it was.'

'What I mean is...' She took a sip of the local red wine Bianca had poured and tried to frame her thoughts. 'You're at home here,' she finally said.

Stefano was quiet for a long moment, his shuttered gaze still on the mountains. 'Yes,' he finally said, and it sounded like a reluctant confession.

Allegra knew better than to press. Not now, not yet.

After lunch Bianca showed Allegra to her room while Stefano went to his home office to deal with business. Allegra took in the wide oak bed and dresser, simple yet adequate furnishings. There was no decoration in the room save a pair of gauzy white curtains framing the only artistry the villa needed, the view outside.

She stood at the window and took several deep, clean lungfuls of air. The scent of pine was sharp, and she heard the lonely bleat of a sheep on a distant hillside.

Stefano's words from this morning reverberated yet again through her mind and her heart. *You want to talk about feelings? What about yours?*

Yes, she had feelings, as much as she longed to deny them even to herself. She didn't like to consider those feelings fermenting inside her—memories, regrets, fears and disappointments. They bubbled up, demanding to be recognised, to be *felt,* and she pushed them down, again and again. It was so much easier not to think.

Not to feel.

She wondered if Stefano was the same. She knew he had things he refused to consider.

Like the fact that he was angry with her. Still. Now. Allegra wasn't sure if he even knew it. Or if knew it, like her, it was simply one more emotion to suppress.

He'd denied it this morning and yet Allegra knew—*knew*—he'd been angry with her last night. Deeply angry, angry in a way he had no right to be.

Her lips twisted in a cynical smile. Of course, Stefano would think he had a right. He'd thought of her as a possession all those years ago, prized perhaps, but an object nonetheless. Something to be owned.

And he was the same now. He'd shown her last night; he thought of her in those terms still.

And it hurt, she knew, because just as he was still the man

he'd been all those years ago, the man who'd coldly asked her, *'What more is there?'* so she was still that same girl, wanting to believe, begging for love.

Allegra closed her eyes. Neither of them had changed as much as they thought they had.

As much as they'd wanted to.

'I want to show you something,' Stefano said. He stood in the doorway, one shoulder propped against the door-frame.

Allegra kept her back to him and spread her arms wide as she gazed out at the vista. 'What more could you show me?'

Stefano laughed softly. 'You like the view?'

'Yes,' Allegra said simply.

'Come with me.'

He had moved behind her, and Allegra could feel his presence, his breath. She resisted the urge to lean back against him. It was a ridiculous urge, she told herself, as ridiculous and inappropriate as her thoughts had been earlier, expecting a miracle.

She felt Stefano's tension vibrating between them, a tension born of an awareness of each other—bodies, minds, memories.

'All right,' she said, and turned around.

Stefano led her down the upstairs corridor and to another bedroom on the southern side of the villa.

'Here.' He opened the door and ushered Allegra in before him. She looked around in surprise.

It wasn't a bedroom; it was a studio. The room had windows on two sides and was flooded with clear, perfect light. It contained everything she could possibly need for her work with Lucio: an easel, sketchbooks, paints and pastels, charcoals and chalks, brushes and pencils and pens. There was a stool by the easel and a comfortable chair in the corner, wrapped in sunlight.

Allegra moved slowly through the room. It was incredibly thoughtful of Stefano to provide it for her and Lucio, yet even now she felt a finger of unease creeping up her spine.

All the art supplies in the world weren't going to make Lucio talk. That, she knew, was one thing Stefano couldn't buy.

He looked around the room in satisfaction. 'I had only the best brought here, flown by helicopter from Rome.' There was a hidden vulnerability in his eyes as he turned to her. 'You like it? It will be enough?'

Looking at him, at the room he'd provided for Lucio with such complete, considering care, Allegra felt her heart contract.

'Stefano, it's amazing.' She crossed over to him and, standing on tiptoe, she kissed his cheek. 'Thank you.'

His eyes flared in surprise, in awareness. 'You're welcome.'

They stood that way for a moment, a hand span apart, and Allegra felt desire and something deeper uncoil in her belly, spiral upwards. She wanted him to take her in his arms. She wanted to go there.

It would have been so easy, so devastatingly easy, to take that one last step towards him, to let him pull her into his arms, brush his lips against hers. She could feel it; she could almost taste it.

She wanted it.

But he didn't take that step, didn't touch her. Of course he didn't. She shouldn't have wanted it; she certainly shouldn't expect it. Not now, not ever.

Stefano gazed down at her, a smile quirking the corner of his mouth without reaching his eyes.

Allegra smiled back and stepped away.

'I'll leave you alone,' Stefano said, moving towards the door. 'I'm sure there are things you need to do, in preparation for your work with Lucio. We usually eat around seven.'

Allegra spent the rest of the afternoon reviewing Lucio's case notes. According to Bianca, he had been napping in the villa when Enzo had died. She'd told him about the accident that night, had always talked about Enzo in warm and loving terms to keep his memory alive. At first, Lucio had responded, grieved, seemed normal. Then slowly he'd begun to withdraw verbally, physically, emotionally.

Over the ensuing months he had retreated further and further into his own safe, silent world. When he was forced out of it, it was as if a switch had been flipped and he became agitated, screaming incoherently, banging his head against the floor or wall.

Bianca had been forced to withdraw him from the nursery in the local village and soon it had become difficult to take him to shops or church. He greeted the world with blank, staring eyes, didn't interact with anyone or anything.

Lost in thought, Allegra gazed out of the window, the sun sinking behind the rugged mountain peaks. While all of Lucio's behaviours fell into the normal spectrum of childhood grief, the length and depth of them did not.

A grieving child should begin to respond to therapy, to improve, even if it was a two steps forward, one step backward type of improvement. Yet Lucio was not improving. He was slowly, steadily growing worse.

Allegra uncurled herself from the chair and wandered around the studio as a settling twilight lengthened the shadows on the floor. She let her fingers drift over the stiff new bristles on the paintbrushes, the untouched paints, unopened packets of crayons and felt-tip pens.

Worry gnawed and nibbled at her insides. She'd come here to help Lucio; that, of course, always, had been her primary goal. Yet now she doubted. What if she couldn't help him? What if he really was autistic?

What if, a little voice whispered inside her heart, she'd really come here for a selfish reason? And what was that reason?

To see Stefano again.

She gave a little, instinctive shake of her head. *No.* Surely not. *Please.*

Yet she couldn't deny that seeing him again had stirred something to life inside her she'd long thought dead. Something she wanted to be dead.

She didn't want to care about Stefano, didn't want to hand him her heart so he could carelessly grind it with his heel.

Do you love me?

No, she wouldn't go there, wouldn't let herself. She'd shut herself off from the past for the last seven years, and she could continue to do so. Love, if that was what this was, was just another emotion to suppress.

Outside, a wolf howled, a distant, lonely sound. It was now nearly completely dark and Allegra realized the hour had to be quite late.

'Allegra?'

She stiffened, turned. Silhouetted against a spill of light from the hallway was Stefano.

'What is it?' she asked, and her voice came out sharper than she meant it to be. She felt rather than saw Stefano stiffen in response, and then saw that reaction resolutely change into a more predictable one: he shrugged.

'Dinner is ready. I thought you'd want to know.' Without waiting for her, he turned and left.

After a few moments, Allegra followed.

Downstairs, the kitchen was warm and cosy, with light and steam from several pots, their savoury contents bubbling merrily. Bianca stood at the sink, scrubbing a pan, while Stefano stood next to her, chopping a tomato for a salad.

They were chatting and laughing like friends, while Lucio stood by the window, methodically tapping the windowsill with a wooden spoon.

Stefano turned his head, caught sight of Allegra, and his eyes blazed into hers for a second before he beckoned her in and then turned back to his chopping.

Yet that moment of intensity struck Allegra to her core, and she wondered if that blaze of feeling had been anger or affection, or something else altogether.

They all ate together in the kitchen. Lucio sat next to Bianca, everything about him sombre and silent, his face and eyes blank. Allegra sat on his other side and, even though he didn't respond to her, she included him in the conversation, smiling and making eye contact as much and as naturally as she could.

Bianca and Stefano chatted easily with her over the meal of pasta with sausage and beans, a simple, hearty speciality of the region.

After dinner, Allegra insisted on helping Bianca with the washing-up. In typical Italian style, Bianca shooed Stefano out of the kitchen.

'We don't want him here anyway,' Bianca said with a mischievous smile. 'Women's work and women's talk, eh?'

Allegra gave a little laugh, choosing not to take offence at the inherent sexism in her remark.

'I'm glad you agreed to help Lucio,' Bianca said as they scraped the plates. 'It can't have been easy, considering.'

'Considering…?' Allegra asked, her eyebrows raised. Bianca's head was bent, her eyes on the dirty dishes in the sink.

'Considering that you and Stefano nearly married,' she said quietly, and Allegra experienced a cold ripple of shock.

'I didn't realize you knew our history,' she said after a moment. Her voice came out calm, normal, and she was glad.

Bianca looked up, surprised. 'Of course I knew. I've known Stefano since I was a baby and he was a boy. When his father died, my own took him in. He's like a brother to me.'

Allegra nodded. At least now she understood Lucio's importance to Stefano, as well as Bianca's.

'I know you had your reasons for leaving,' Bianca continued quietly, 'and I expect they are good ones—'

'Yes,' Allegra couldn't help but interject, 'they are. Were.' She turned to the table to collect more dishes. 'Stefano and I have agreed to put the past behind us. It's best for Lucio and, frankly, I think it's best for us.'

'Easier said than done,' Bianca said quietly.

Allegra turned around. 'What do you mean?'

'I see the way he looks at you,' Bianca replied with a shrug. 'He loved you then, and I wonder if he perhaps loves you still.'

The remark, made with such stark simplicity, caused Allegra to give a short laugh of disbelief. 'Bianca, Stefano never loved me! He told me as much. And I am quite certain he doesn't love me now. We…we don't really know each other any more. I don't think we ever did.'

Bianca shrugged again. 'If that is easier to believe…'

'It's easier to believe,' Allegra replied, 'because it's the truth. Trust me. Stefano never loved me, never even considered loving me, and he's made that clear many, many times.'

'But,' Bianca surmised softly, 'you love him.'

Allegra's breath came out in a short, surprised rush. 'No,' she said, and heard the doubt in her own voice. Her horrified gaze lifted to meet Bianca's knowing one. 'No!' She shook her head. 'No, I did love him—terribly—seven years ago. But now? No.' Another shake of her head, and her voice came out firm, strident. 'No, I don't,' she continued, talking as much to herself as to Bianca. 'Of course, seeing him again is bound to make me remember—feel—certain things, but no.' Now she met Bianca's sombre smile, her own smile dazzling, determined in its certainty. 'No, I don't love him,' she stated with a strange triumph, and her heart sank as Bianca merely smiled, shrugging in a way that managed to convey her scepticism and sympathy without saying a word.

After the dishes were done, Bianca went to put Lucio to bed and Allegra wandered through the darkened, empty rooms of the villa until she came to the lounge. The double doors were only partly ajar and warm light spilled from within.

She peeped inside, saw Stefano in an overstuffed armchair, intent on reading an old leather-bound book. She realized with a little jolt that he wore reading glasses. This tiny weakness made him somehow more approachable, and she stepped inside.

Stefano looked up and smiled briefly, coolly. 'All right?'

'Yes. I'm all right. Bianca's putting Lucio to bed.'

'Good.'

She came further into the room, perched on the edge of a sofa. The room was cosy and warm, decorated in warm red fabrics and mahogany, a haven against the unrelenting darkness outside.

'Do you think Bianca will marry again?' she asked.

Stefano glanced up. 'Perhaps, in time. There are not many men out here, though.' He smiled faintly. 'You saw the pickings in town, at the café.'

'Yes.' She paused, looked at him. 'Bianca mentioned that you lived with her family when your father died.'

Stefano stilled, the expression in his eyes shadowed, hidden. Allegra saw his long tapered fingers tense on the cover of his book.

'Yes, I did.'

'What happened to your family?' Allegra asked. 'Your mother, your brothers and sisters?'

'They went elsewhere.'

She shook her head, confused. 'Why?'

'Why are you asking these questions, Allegra?' There was a wary sharpness to his tone and Allegra faced it.

'Because I realize I should have asked them before. I should have thought to ask them, wanted to ask them.'

'Before?'

'When we were engaged. When I was nineteen.'

Stefano took off his reading glasses. He was silent for a moment, his head bent, his expression hidden. Then he looked up and smiled mockingly. 'Having regrets, Allegra?' he asked softly.

'No,' she retorted, still buoyed by her conviction earlier. 'No, of course not. I'll never regret what I did, Stefano, because it was the right thing to do. We would have made a terrible couple.'

His mouth twisted. 'Then why do you care?'

'It's called making conversation.' She lifted her chin, held her breath and waited.

Stefano was silent for a long moment. His fingers tapped a staccato rhythm on the cover of his book and then he let out a short bark of laughter.

'All right, *fiorina*,' he said, and it sounded like a taunt. 'You want to know? My father died when I was twelve. My family had no money, nothing, and so we were all farmed out while my mother went to work in Naples at a firework factory. Bianca's father took me in, and I was fortunate.'

'What about your sisters?' Allegra whispered.

'Elizabetta went with my mother, to Naples, and died in a factory accident. Rosalia stayed with an aunt in Abruzzo, met a mechanic and married. She's happy the way she is, hasn't wanted anything from me.' A quick, short shrug. 'And little Bella, who was younger than me, she did okay until I started giving her money, sent her to boarding school, gave her the means to better herself, and all it did was finance a drug habit that eventually killed her.' His smile was cold, a coldness that seeped straight into Allegra's soul. 'So that's my family history. Satisfied?' And, without another thought, he flipped open his book, readjusted his glasses and began to read.

Allegra stared at him, her heart aching. No, she was not satisfied. Not in the least.

Slowly she walked towards him and laid a hand on the page of his book. Stefano stilled again. 'Why did you never tell me this before?'

'When was I to mention it?' Stefano asked in a disbelieving drawl. 'It's not the kind of pedigree that would have impressed your parents, or you for that matter.'

'Still…'

He looked up, his mouth twisting in mockery. 'Did you really want to know, Allegra? Or did you want to keep believing that I was the dashing prince you thought me to be?'

She shook her head. 'No, Stefano, I wanted to know the real you. I loved you—'

'You loved the man you thought I was.' Stefano cut her off with cruel, cutting precision. 'And when you learned I wasn't, that my feet were made of clay, you hightailed it to England. So spare me all the misunderstood melodrama now, please.' With two fingers he removed her hand as if it were something slimy and distasteful and it fell helplessly to Allegra's side.

She stood there, feeling the shock waves pulse painfully

through her. Stefano's assessment had been so cold, so cruel, so *clear*. There could be no doubt now what he thought of her…what he'd always thought of her.

Stefano closed his book. 'I'm leaving tomorrow,' he announced in a neutral voice. Allegra's startled gaze flew to his. He met her gaze with a stare as blank as Lucio's.

'Tomorrow? Why so soon?'

'It's for the best, don't you think? I don't want to distract you from your work with Lucio.'

Allegra nodded, accepting that Stefano would be a hopeless distraction, as much as she didn't want him to be.

'When will you return?' she asked and he shrugged.

'I don't know,' he replied. He sounded so casual, so indifferent, that Allegra was stung.

'Very well,' she said, trying to match his tone, his shrug. Stefano smiled faintly. He laid his book on the table and rose, closing the small space between them in just a few steps.

He stood before her, reached out to tuck a tendril of hair behind her ear before drifting his hand along her cheek. It was a gesture born of tenderness, like a phoenix rising from the ashes of his earlier anger.

Allegra looked up at him, saw not anger in his eyes but sorrow. Grief.

'It's better this way, *fiorina*,' he whispered. 'For both of us.' Lightly—so lightly—he rested his forehead against hers. Allegra felt his breath stir her hair, felt the sorrow and regret that wrapped them both in a fog of feeling.

She wanted to speak, opened her mouth, but all that came out was a tiny choked cry, as feeble and useless as a baby bird's. Silently, she reached up and touched Stefano's fingers, pressing them against her cheek before he tugged his hand gently from hers and stepped away.

'Goodnight,' he murmured, and walked out of the room, leaving her there with the darkness and the memories.

CHAPTER EIGHT

THE SUN WAS streaming through the wide windows when Allegra awoke. She lay in bed, waiting for memories and feelings to catch up and play havoc with her heart.

She thought of Stefano's assessment of her love, herself, and still felt stung, stunned. Then she remembered his sad smile, a smile that had cut through her defences in a single stroke and left her wondering.

She threw off the covers and jumped out of bed, showering and dressing quickly. She couldn't think of Stefano; she needed to concentrate on Lucio. He was the reason—the only reason—she was here.

The villa was surprisingly quiet as she came downstairs. She saw Bianca in the kitchen, washing dishes. Lucio was at the table, running a toy car methodically along its wooden surface.

'Bianca?' Allegra stepped into the welcoming warmth, instinctively looking for Stefano.

'Stefano went back to Rome,' Bianca said. 'Early this morning.'

Allegra nodded. She'd known he was leaving, of course, and yet she'd wanted to say goodbye. Perhaps they had said goodbye last night. It had, in a way, felt like a farewell.

'He said he had business there,' Bianca continued, a knowing compassion in her dark eyes. 'He'll be back in a few weeks.'

A few weeks. Allegra nodded, tried to smile. It was for the best, she knew. 'Can I help with breakfast?' she asked.

'No, no, it's all made,' Bianca said, and served Allegra with cappuccino and pastries.

After breakfast, Bianca left for another part of the house and Allegra began her work with Lucio. She intended to spend the first few days simply observing him, allowing Lucio to become accustomed to her presence. He didn't even look at her as he played, running his car over and over again along the table's surface, his expression blank and fixated on the seemingly mindless activity.

After a few minutes of this, Allegra began to talk, making friendly, interested comments about his car, the house, the view of mountains outside. She didn't expect answers, only waited a few seconds for them before she continued cheerfully. Lucio didn't even look her way, but at least he tolerated her presence.

The next few days continued in much the same way. Lucio allowed Allegra to be in the same room with him, played his mindless, methodical games while she sat next to him and chatted. But he never looked at her, never responded in any way, and Allegra had to admit to herself that she was discouraged.

One evening after Lucio had gone to bed, Bianca approached her. 'Is it not working?' she asked, her fingers knotted together, her eyes filled with disappointed sorrow.

Allegra, curled up on the sofa in the lounge, looked up from the notes she'd been studying. 'It's not a question of whether it's working or not, Bianca,' she explained quietly. 'Lucio needs time. I don't want to begin proper therapy with him until he's comfortable with me.'

Bianca nodded. 'It's hard to wait.'

'Of course it is,' Allegra agreed. She touched Bianca's hand. 'You know, though, that Lucio may indeed be autistic? Even though that is a diagnosis that is difficult for any parent to accept, especially if their child did once have speech and other behaviours that would contradict such a diagnosis. Still, it's a possibility.'

Bianca swallowed. 'I know.'

'I'll do my best,' Allegra promised, 'but if his silence and other behaviours are trauma induced, then it's likely we're missing something. His level of emotional suppression is severe and extraordinary.' She paused, letting Bianca take a moment to digest this. Then she asked, 'Have you tried speaking with Lucio about his father? I know sometimes it seems easier—and kinder—not to talk about it, but Lucio needs an outlet for his feelings.'

'I talked with him at first,' Bianca said. 'But he would grow agitated and I didn't want to upset him. Then he started just to fall silent instead and, as you know, it worsened until he wasn't speaking or even responding at all.' She bit her lip. 'It was hard for me too—talking about Enzo.'

'Of course it was,' Allegra murmured.

'Lucio always loved to draw, though,' Bianca said and, although her voice wobbled, there was hope in her eyes. 'When Stefano mentioned the idea of art therapy, even without the experience you've had with a child like Lucio, I felt encouraged. He hasn't drawn anything since he stopped speaking, but if you help him…guide him…' She trailed off, looking to Allegra for reassurance, comfort.

Allegra smiled. She was used to the conflicting mixture of scepticism and hope, the intense desire for change coupled with the disbelief that it could ever happen.

She felt that way about Stefano. The thought shocked her. She and Stefano didn't even have a relationship. They'd agreed to keep their distance.

And yet. And yet.

She couldn't deny her own feelings resurfacing after all these years, still wanting something he couldn't give her.

Love.

The kind of love she needed, wanted.

'I'm sorry,' Allegra said after a moment, realizing her thoughts had scattered, her mind spinning. 'Yes, I think art could help Lucio. But whether or not it's the key that unlocks his silence…' she shrugged, smiling sadly, '…only time will tell.' Allegra reached over to cover Bianca's hand with her own. 'I'll do my best to reach him, Bianca,' she said softly, and the other woman's eyes shone with unshed tears.

'It hurts,' she said simply, 'to love.'

Yes, it did, Allegra knew. It hurt when your dreams were disappointed, your hopes crushed.

It hurt so much.

And was Stefano hurt? The question whispered through her mind, her heart, as it had in the days since he'd left.

Was he angry because his pride was hurt, or was it something more? Something deeper?

And why, Allegra wondered hopelessly, did she want it to be?

The next day Allegra took Lucio to the art studio upstairs. He was surprisingly docile, allowing her to lead him down the corridor and into the room, the pale floorboards washed in the morning sunlight. He stood in the middle of the room, his eyes flickering around the art materials before coming to a rest, gazing out at a mindless middle distance.

'Stefano told me you like art,' Allegra said. 'He has some of your drawings by his desk. Do you like to draw with crayons?' She sat on the floor in the middle of the room and took a handful of crayons from a plastic tub.

She named the colours one by one, let them fall through her fingers. Lucio watched, silent, his eyes flickering over the crayons.

'Would you like to draw?' Allegra asked gently. She took a wide white sheet of paper and laid it in front of him and waited.

Lucio stared at the blank paper for a long moment and then looked away.

Still Allegra persevered, chatting easily. She drew a few streaks of colour to show him, not wanting to guide or influence him too much, but still Lucio did nothing, said nothing.

They stopped at lunch time and Lucio followed her silently down to the kitchen. Allegra felt the heavy burden of disappointment and helplessness. She wasn't reaching Lucio, just as no one had been able to reach him.

Most children she worked with weren't nearly as trauma-tised as Lucio was, if it was indeed trauma that was causing his silence. The children she usually encountered were more than willing to scribble with felt-tips, pound clay, splatter paint. Allegra facilitated their creativity, helped them work through their emotions by helping them expand and complete their pictures.

She wasn't used to this—stone walls of silence, blank stares, *nothing*. Lucio was giving her nothing to work with, and she realized she felt completely out of her depth.

He needed an experienced psychiatrist or grief counsellor, not an art therapist who had only been qualified for two years. Yet she couldn't abandon Lucio now, even if she wanted to, which she didn't.

Still, Allegra resolved, when Stefano returned she would impress upon him the importance of entrusting Lucio's care to additional professionals.

It was not a job she could manage on her own, and she felt the burden of both Bianca and Stefano's expectation and hope weigh heavily on her.

That evening, after Lucio was in bed, Bianca came into the lounge where Allegra was reading. 'The telephone,' she said, holding out the receiver. 'It is Stefano, for you.'

Allegra's heart tumbled over. She smiled, murmured her thanks and took the phone. Bianca withdrew.

'Hello?'

'Allegra.'

She was surprised to hear the emotion in his voice—what was it? Relief, perhaps, and regret. Something unfathomable and deep.

'Hello, Stefano,' she said quietly.

'How are things progressing with Lucio?' he asked, revert-ing to a more impersonal tone.

'Slowly. You can't expect much yet. It's early days.'

'No words?'

'No. But I wouldn't judge success by his ability to speak,

Stefano. If suppressed trauma is indeed the cause of his symptoms, he needs to remember first. And feel. He hasn't grieved properly and he needs to.'

'How,' Stefano murmured, 'do you allow someone to grieve?'

'Give him a safe place to express himself,' Allegra replied quietly. 'Lucio is an extreme case, I'll confess.' She paused before continuing carefully. 'I don't think we can rule out an autism diagnosis.'

Stefano let out a short, sharp breath before saying evenly, 'You've been with him less than a week.'

'I know that,' Allegra said, 'but I also want to make sure you and Bianca understand what to expect…or not to expect.'

'Barring autism, what do you think could be the source of his trauma?'

Allegra nibbled her lower lip, thinking. She'd given this very question a great deal of thought over the last few days, wondering what secret or surprise Lucio was withholding, perhaps without even knowing it. 'I almost wonder,' she said slowly, 'if there isn't something more that he's suppressing, something none of us knows about.'

'Like what?' Allegra heard the bite of impatience in Stefano's voice and knew that, like Bianca, he was disappointed and frustrated.

No matter what she'd said, he wanted answers. Miracles.

'Something about Enzo's death?' Allegra guessed. 'It could be anything. If he saw Enzo—'

'Impossible. Bianca said he was asleep.'

'Perhaps he overheard something, then,' Allegra suggested. 'A small child can easily take adult remarks out of context and apportion blame to himself—'

'You think he blames himself for his father's death?' Stefano asked, and she heard the incredulity in his voice.

'I don't know,' she replied, struggling to keep her own voice quiet and even.

'Well, find out,' Stefano snapped and then, before Allegra

could frame a reply, he sighed and said, 'I'm sorry. I know you are doing all you can.'

'I'm trying,' she whispered and they were both silent, listening to each other's breathing. There were other things Allegra wanted to say, things that had nothing to do with Lucio and all to do with her and Stefano.

Yet she didn't even know where to begin. She didn't even know what to *feel.* And neither, it seemed, did Stefano, for he too remained silent; both of them quiet and listening without speaking a word.

They should have said goodbye, should have said *something,* but neither of them did.

The phone wire provided a strange, intimate connection between them. A temporary connection, for after that endless, aching moment, Stefano said quietly, 'Goodnight, Allegra,' and severed it.

The next morning Allegra took Lucio to the art studio again. She tried clay, finger-paints and crayons, but he showed no interest.

Deciding to take a different approach, Allegra drew a picture for him.

'This is the view from my window,' she said, smiling, as she drew a simple scene of mountains, sun and sky. 'I love looking at it every morning.' She held it out to him. 'Is there anything you'd add to that picture, Lucio? What do you see when you look out of the window?'

Lucio stared at the picture for a long moment—long enough for Allegra's arms to ache and she almost put it down. Then he looked down at the crayons and she held her breath.

Lucio picked a black crayon and took the picture. Then, systematically, as methodically as he'd done everything else, he drew with the black crayon, not stopping until the entire drawing was covered in blackness.

She watched him draw, watched the fierce concentration on his face, made more pitiable by his complete silence.

She looked down at the picture. In places the paper had ripped from the force of his crayon.

He'd made an astonishing statement; he'd communicated. And the message was clear—clear and terrible.

Lucio was trapped, she thought, trapped and tormented by suppressed memories and emotions—emotions that held him in their snare and refused to let him go, just as he couldn't let go of them.

Just as she and Stefano couldn't.

Allegra put the blackened drawing aside and gently laid her hand on Lucio's shoulder. He didn't flinch, didn't move.

'When my father died,' Allegra said quietly, 'I sometimes felt empty inside, as if there was nothing inside of me. And, other times, I felt so *full,* as if I was going to explode if I didn't do something. But I never knew what to do.'

She waited, letting Lucio hear what she was saying, allowing it to filter through his consciousness. Then she retrieved a lump of clay and put it on the floor between them.

'Would you like to make something with the clay?' she asked gently. 'Squish it between your fingers, if you like. It's soft.'

After a long silent moment Lucio reached out and touched the clay, stroked it with one finger. Then he dropped his hand. Allegra knew they'd done enough for one day.

'We can work with the clay tomorrow, if you like,' she said and, standing up, led Lucio from the room.

Late that afternoon, when the peak of Gran Sasso was touched with gold, Allegra took a walk down the front drive. Bianca had taken Lucio with her to collect eggs from the hen house, encouraged by the small step, awful as it had been, that Lucio had taken. Allegra was grateful for a few moments' relaxation.

The wind whispered through the oak trees, their leaves already touched with a deep, mellow gold. In the distance a cow lowed mournfully and she heard the tinkling of its bell.

It was peaceful here, she realized, even though concern for

Lucio overshadowed that sense of serenity. She was glad there was a crack of communication in the walls he'd built around himself, relieved that it indicated he might not be autistic. Yet she was also intimidated by the depth of Lucio's trauma, and the amount of work that would have to be done to help him recover—work she could not do on her own.

Yet today the realization of his hidden hurt and anger, a terrible grief he'd suppressed so completely, made her conscious of her own veiled emotions in a way she'd never been before.

She'd always known that she didn't think about her former life, ended so abruptly the night she'd run away. She'd quite consciously put those memories in a box, had done it on purpose as a way to build her own future. Yet she hadn't realized that those memories held so much pain—pain and hurt, fear and guilt.

She hadn't realized until Stefano had come back into her life, forcing her to confront not just the past, but her own self. The girl she'd been, the woman she was.

Am I so different? Have I changed?

She'd spent the last seven years rushing, straining, trying to prove herself in a thousand different ways and here she found herself resting at last.

It was hard to let go of that sense of urgent striving, hard to let the cares and worries tumble from her. Her heart and mind resisted, her body tensed. She wanted to keep it all at bay and yet she couldn't.

She couldn't…she was afraid of what might happen when she finally let it all go.

Something black flashed between the trees and after a moment Allegra saw what it was: Stefano's car. She stood uncertainly by the side of the road and watched as the vehicle, and Stefano, drew closer to her, finally slowing to a stop right in front of her.

Stefano climbed out, stood with one hand resting on the bonnet of the car, his eyes fathomless, his face blank.

'What are you doing?' he asked.

She shrugged. 'Going for a walk.'

'What about Lucio?'

She flushed at the implication that she was neglecting her responsibility. 'He's with Bianca. We had a productive session this morning.'

'Did you?'

'Yes.'

'Is he speaking?'

'I told you, it's not that simple, Stefano. He isn't just going to magically start talking and be better.'

Stefano ran a hand over his face and Allegra realized how tired he looked.

'You're back,' she stated unnecessarily. 'Why?'

'I wanted to see how Lucio was doing.'

Allegra nodded, swallowed. Of course, that was to be expected. She was disappointed, delusional, to think he'd wanted to see her.

Stefano's gaze slid away from hers, resting among a copse of trees by the twisting road. 'I haven't been down here in a while,' he said.

Allegra didn't know what he meant—they were standing on the main drive, after all—when she saw Stefano start to walk towards the trees.

She looked over her shoulder and saw the dilapidated structure huddled in a copse of elms—the building she'd seen when they'd first arrived.

Stefano walked towards it, mindless of the long grass catching on his finely tailored suit.

Wary and intrigued, Allegra followed him.

He stopped in front of the hovel. The timbers were rotting, the windows gaping, shutters askew. Most of the roof had fallen in and terracotta tiles lay scattered around. A stunted sapling grew determinedly through the hole in the roof.

'I haven't been over here in years,' Stefano said, half to himself. 'I'm not sure it's safe to go inside.'

Allegra was inclined to agree, but Stefano still moved forward, picking his way through the fallen stone, the rotting timber, and ducked his head under the low lintel.

'Stefano…?' she asked uncertainly. She had no idea why he was here, what he was thinking.

Dusk was falling; the peak of Gran Sasso, touched with gold only moments before, was now cloaked in darkness. A chill had crept into the air, wound its way through the mountains, into Allegra's bones.

Stefano appeared in the doorway. 'This is my home,' he said simply. It took Allegra a moment to understand.

This was his home. This falling-down two-room hovel. This.

Allegra surveyed the tumbled stone and rotting wood. 'You grew up here?' she asked, trying not to sound incredulous.

'I told you the other night my family had nothing.'

Allegra swallowed. 'I know. I just didn't think—'

He laughed. 'That I was *this* poor? Well, I was. Believe it.' There was a savage note to his voice as he added, 'I worked hard to lose my country accent, my country manners.'

'You succeeded,' she said with a small smile, but there was pain in her heart, a pain she saw reflected in Stefano's eyes. 'Tell me,' she said.

Stefano gave a little shrug. 'My father was a farmer. We had a few sheep, a couple of cows. Then the agricultural industry collapsed in this region and my father left our farm to seek work in the mines in Wallonia, in Belgium.'

'You work in the mining industry now,' Allegra said after a moment. She felt as if she'd been given a handful of scattered puzzle pieces and she had to work out where they fitted.

'Yes.' Stefano paused. 'My father died in a mining accident. When I started my business, one of my goals was to make machinery that would keep miners safe, keep men like my father from dying needlessly.' He smiled, although his voice was hard and held no humour. 'It also happened to make me rich.'

They were both silent, listening to the creak of the trees, the slap of a loose shutter in the wind.

Allegra thought of her mother's words, *Your social connections, his money,* and it made sense, a horrible sense when she realized just how important, how necessary those social connections must have been.

'I suppose,' she said slowly, 'for business, it would help to be socially connected.'

Stefano's gaze flicked to her face and he nodded, understanding where her trail of tangled thoughts had led her.

'Yes. There were plenty of men in Milan and other cities who wouldn't do business with me because I didn't have their manners, didn't go to their schools and clubs. I was a rough country boy and they knew it. No matter how much I tried to hide it from them…from you.'

The last came out as a confession and his gaze slid away from hers once more, resting on the distant darkened hills.

'Why?' Allegra met his gaze, searched it. 'Why hide how far you've come? Who you are? You should be *proud*.'

Stefano smiled faintly. 'I'm glad you think so.' He lapsed into silence, lost in thought, one hand resting on the cracked lintel of his family home. 'When my father went to work in the mines,' he began after a moment, his gaze still averted from hers, 'my mother didn't want him to go. She'd heard about the kind of work there. It's a hard life.' He paused, ran his hand down the rough-hewn stone. 'But he went because he knew it was the only way of providing for his family. The only way,' he said, 'of loving them.' He spoke flatly, matter-of-factly. There would be no arguing with that sentiment, Allegra knew. No dispute.

She gazed at him, lost in shadow, in darkness, and understood how much Stefano had revealed with that statement, had revealed it without even realizing.

'And he died there,' she said quietly. He nodded.

'Yes, three years after he went. In all that time, he never came home. He didn't want to waste the money on the train fare.'

There was no regret in Stefano's voice, no anger or hurt or sorrow. There was only fierce, unrelenting pride.

'Didn't your mother miss him?' Allegra asked in a whisper. 'Didn't she want to see him? Didn't he want to see her?'

'Yes,' Stefano said, the conviction in his voice still unshakeable, 'but it didn't matter. He was providing for her, Allegra. He was doing what needed to be done…because he loved her.'

Allegra stared unseeingly at the darkness that cloaked the mountains outside, a darkness that was not pierced by a single light or hope.

What more is there?

Now she understood what he'd meant that awful, never-ending night. She'd known how he loved, but she hadn't realized why. She hadn't understood what it meant, that it could mean *anything*.

She'd said his love was worthless, yet now she realized that perhaps it wasn't.

It wasn't worthless. It just wasn't enough.

How could two people who had loved each other not have been able to find happiness together?

And now? she wondered. Could they still? The question was pointless; Stefano didn't love her any more. And she wasn't willing to ask herself if she loved him. She couldn't think that much—feel that much—yet. Not when her heart was already overflowing, her barriers breaking. Not when it was getting so desperately difficult to hold everything back, at bay.

They walked back to the villa in the dark, in silence. Warm light spilled from the windows. While Stefano went to check his messages, Allegra decided to see if she could help Bianca in the kitchen.

Dinner was a surprisingly cheerful, chatty affair, and it felt right to have Stefano among them again. Yet still Allegra felt the undercurrents of tension, of remembrance, pulling at her own heart.

She saw Stefano glance at her, an understanding and knowledge in his eyes that made her own gaze slide away.

Everything was conspiring to make her think, make her feel. Perhaps it was being in the mountains, perhaps it was seeing Stefano again, perhaps it was the intensive work she was doing with Lucio, so different from her weekly sessions with a dozen different patients.

Now she found those barriers cracking completely, the memories and feelings threatening to rush over and engulf her. And, strangest of all, she found herself wanting it. Craving it, needing it.

She wanted to open the box she'd closed all those years ago and scatter the feelings and fears to this clean, healing wind.

She just didn't know how to begin. How to prise open the lid, how to deal with the questions. The memories.

The feelings.

Later, when Bianca was putting Lucio to bed, Allegra went upstairs to the art studio. It was shrouded in darkness, the only light coming from a spill of moonlight through the wide windows.

Allegra sat on a stool, ran her fingers over the drawing Lucio had blackened. Its desecration had been the first key to his healing.

Yet it was not his healing she was reflecting on now, but her own. She felt an ache, deep within, of sorrow and regret, loss and grief. It was an ache she'd become accustomed to; it had become a part of her own self, dull, and steady, so easy to ignore.

Yet now she felt it rise up in her chest, threaten to erupt in a never-ending howl of misery that she couldn't deal with on her own. Couldn't accept.

She bowed her head, willing the tears, the pain back.

She'd almost succeeded, felt her eyes become dry and gritty, her throat sore and aching with effort, when she heard a sound at the door.

'Allegra.'

She gave a tiny shake of her head, her hair tumbling over her shoulders, shrouding her face in a tangle. She couldn't bear it if Stefano was kind now; she couldn't bear to feel anything more.

He walked into the room, laid a strong hand on her shoulder.

'Don't,' Allegra pleaded in a tiny whisper. 'I can't…'

'Yes,' Stefano said, 'you can.'

She closed her eyes, clenched her fists. *No.* She wouldn't cry. She wouldn't cry in front of Stefano; she couldn't let him see all the pain and the hurt, the *mess* that was inside her. She couldn't show him how little she'd changed from the girl he'd known, the girl who had loved him so utterly, so uncontrollably…

No.

Stefano crouched down, his face level with hers although Allegra still didn't—couldn't—look at him, her hair tangling against her flushed cheeks and thankfully obscuring her vision.

Stefano's hand was still on her shoulder and with his other hand he cupped her cheek. Allegra let out a little choked cry, tried to resist as he slowly, inexorably, drew her to him.

His chest was hard and solid against her cheek, and she found herself nestling against his shoulder, her lips pressed to the hollow of his throat.

And then it came, the tide of sorrow she'd willed back for so many years, the tears she'd refused to shed or even acknowledge.

Her shoulders shook with the force of her sobs, shook her with silent, healing tremors.

She felt as if she should stop, and once she tried to pull back, to get herself under control, but Stefano wouldn't let her. He held her to him, his arms gentle yet strong, but instead of a prison it had become a sanctuary.

She felt safe. Safe and loved, protected and provided for in a way she'd never dreamed of, had never imagined possible.

Protection. Provision.

And still she cried, tears streaming down her cheeks, running into her nose and mouth, dampening her hair. She was a mess, inside and out, an open, unlovely, desperate mess, and she didn't care.

Stefano didn't care.

She'd held herself together for so long and now all the pieces were coming unstuck, the lid of that box blown clear off.

She didn't know how long she cried—a few minutes, an hour?—but eventually the tears subsided, and her body relaxed, sagged against Stefano.

He was seated on the floor, cradling her like a child, washed in moonlight.

They didn't speak for a long time. Allegra listened to the silence, heard the quiet rasp of their breathing, the beating of their hearts. Outside, darkness had settled like a cloak of velvet and she heard a wolf give a long, lonely howl.

She didn't know what to say. She wanted to apologise, but she resisted the urge to explain away what had happened or, worse, to pretend that it hadn't happened at all.

'Thank you,' she finally whispered, and Stefano smoothed her hair back from her face, tilting her chin so that their eyes met. She couldn't quite see his expression in the darkness, but she felt it.

Felt the compassion and tenderness emanating from him in warm, engulfing waves.

'How is it,' he murmured softly, 'that a woman who has dedicated her life to helping children uncover their emotions has hid hers away for so long?'

Allegra gave a trembling laugh. 'I don't know. I suppose I knew I was doing it, but I didn't…I didn't realize quite how much.'

Stefano continued to smooth her hair with careful, gentle hands. 'Tell me,' he said quietly, 'what you were crying for.'

'Everything,' Allegra whispered. Yet she knew she couldn't leave it there, knew she had to explain. Explain everything. 'For my father,' she began slowly, feeling the words, feeling her heart wrap around them. 'For how he used me, and how I know I hurt him. If I'd known he'd made so many investments, needed the money…I…'

'You would have married me?' Stefano queried gently. '*Fiorina,* it wasn't your fault. You cannot blame yourself for your father's death.'

'I know that,' Allegra said. 'At least, in my head. But my heart…'

'We can't always control our hearts,' Stefano murmured wryly.

'No. It's been easier not to think of it. To simply not think of it at all.'

'And his funeral?'

'It was too hard,' Allegra said simply. 'So I left. But it still hurt. It always hurts.'

Stefano nodded, stroking her hair. 'Yes,' he murmured, 'of course it does.'

'And my mother,' Allegra continued, quieter, calmer now. 'I know she used me. I realized it as soon as she left my father and took up with Alfonso. He was the one who drove me to the train! She wanted only to humiliate my father, and I was a means to that end, nothing more. Never anything more.' She shook her head, still cradled in Stefano's arms. 'Yet it still hurts,' she whispered. 'It hurts that I was nothing but a bargaining chip to them…' She trailed off, unsure if she should— could—continue. Stefano waited, stroking her hair, her cheek. 'And it hurts,' Allegra finally said, her voice little more than a thread of sound, 'to think that that's all I was to you. You, whom I loved most of all.'

Stefano's hands stilled, tightened, then continued their stroking.

Allegra pressed her face against his shoulder, seeking comfort from the one who had hurt her, the one who now could offer her the healing she needed. 'I loved you so much,' she whispered, her voice choking on the words, the memories. 'And that last night, when we spoke, you…you treated me like a naughty child. Like a possession, a prop. You looked at me as if I were an annoyance to you, and it felt…it felt…*horrible*.' She closed her eyes, squeezed them shut, and still Stefano said nothing. 'Worst of all,' she continued after a moment, 'is the thought, the possibility, that I made a mistake all those years ago. That perhaps I shouldn't have walked—run—away. It torments me now, the thought of what might have happened if I'd stayed.'

Stefano's arms tightened around her. 'Allegra,' he said, his voice roughened with emotion, 'you cannot think about the what-ifs. We were different people then…'

'Were we?' she whispered. '*Were we?*'

'I wouldn't have made you happy,' Stefano said after a long moment, and she heard the regret as well as the certainty in his voice and knew he spoke the truth.

He couldn't have made her happy then, couldn't have been the man she needed.

But now…? Was he the man she needed now?

Slowly Allegra tilted her head until their eyes met. Stefano held her gaze for an endless moment, his eyes searching hers.

Then his lips came down and brushed hers in the barest question of a kiss.

Allegra answered. She answered with her lips, her heart, her whole body. Her arms came around his shoulders, bringing him to her, needing his closeness, his warmth, his strength. Stefano kissed her with a sweet tenderness that shook her to her soul, her very marrow. His tongue gently explored the contours of her lips, her teeth, her mouth, and she clung to him, wanting him, needing him, needing *this*.

His touch was a balm, a blessing, and she felt herself opening up in response, blossoming like the most beautiful and precious of flowers.

Stefano broke the kiss for the barest moment, took a breath, and, lit by a sliver of moonlight, their eyes met, clashed, and something changed.

It was the space of a heartbeat or a breath, yet it felt endless. Stefano kissed her again and this time it was urgent, demanding, angry.

What had been sweet turned savage, a gentle yearning metastasizing into reckless craving.

Stefano's mouth turned hard against hers and her own hands curled into claws, bunching on his arms as fabric pulled and buttons broke and scattered.

Somehow the jar of paintbrushes was knocked to the floor and Allegra distantly heard the shattering of glass, felt a hard brush poking into her back.

How had this happened? she wondered dizzily, even as she answered Stefano kiss for kiss, each touch a brand, as if they were in a desperate race to possess one another, to punish as well as to pleasure.

Desire coursed through her, desire and anger and hurt, all flowing together into one rushing river of emotion. She felt her hands smooth Stefano's bare chest, felt her fingers curl inward, sharp, digging. She heard Stefano's surprised gasp of both pleasure and pain, and laughed aloud with a strange sense of victory.

He pushed her back, his face savage with desire as he pulled her shirt up, lowered his head. She gasped now too, her hands fisted in his hair.

His hands found her, fingers seeking, blazing along her bare skin, touching her in a way she'd never been touched and she gasped as she felt his hand on her breast, her navel, and lower still—so knowing, so intimate, so…

Wrong. This was wrong. She didn't want it like this—on the floor, hard and angry and urgent. They were both angry and they *wanted* to hurt each other.

The thought was horrible, humiliating.

How could you love someone and feel this way? How could you love someone and act this way?

You couldn't. Surely you couldn't.

Her hands stilled, her heart heavy. She didn't want Stefano to look at her, didn't want to see the pain in his eyes, didn't want to feel it in her own heart.

Yet she wanted him—*him*—the man who had hurt her, the man who could heal her.

'Stefano…' she whispered, and choked on the sound. He paused, poised above her, his own expression ravaged, his breathing ragged. They stared at each other for a long moment and then Allegra reached up and cupped his face, felt the rough stubble against her fingers.

Stefano let out a choked cry and rolled away from her, mindless of the broken glass crunching beneath him, one arm thrown over his face.

Broken. Everything felt broken.

Lying there, her clothing in disarray, her dignity in shreds, Allegra wondered if she'd imagined the tenderness, the understanding that had existed between them only moments ago. Now all she felt, all she knew, was anger and pain, hurt and fear.

And then, in the stillness of the shattered night, she heard another sound—a sound that chilled her, made her bolt upright.

Lucio was screaming.

CHAPTER NINE

ALLEGRA STRUGGLED UPWARDS, pulling her clothing to order even as Stefano did the same.

'Lucio—' she said, an explanation, and he nodded.

Stefano hurried down the corridor to Bianca and Lucio's rooms, the little boy's shrill cries still renting the air.

It was a constant, appalling, almost inhuman sound, the sound of an animal in desperate anguish.

Stefano stopped at the threshold of Lucio's room. Bianca sat on his bed, trying to cradle and comfort her thrashing child.

'Lucio,' she begged, tears streaming down her face, 'Lucio, please, it's Mama. *Mama.* Let me hold you—'

It was as if he couldn't hear her. His face was a blank mask of terror, tears streaming from his eyes, his mouth opened in a wide 'O' of endless fear and memory.

Bianca reached to hold him, but he pushed her away, his arms flailing so violently that she would have fallen off the bed if Stefano had not moved forward to steady her.

'Lucio—' Bianca tried again, sobbing.

It was a scene from hell, a scene of personal devastation and torment. There was no healing for Lucio here, Allegra thought, nothing but the overwhelming sense of his own grief and fear.

'Do something,' Stefano said in a jagged voice, and Allegra moved forward.

She sat next to Lucio on the bed, laid a hand on his trembling, jerking shoulder. With her other hand she caught his flailing fist and firmly but gently returned it to his lap, where it continued to shake.

'It's all right, Lucio,' she said in a quiet voice. 'It's all right to feel like this. It's all right to be scared. To be sad. It's *all right*.' Lucio tensed, his body still quivering, and Allegra motioned to Bianca to put her arms around him. 'It's all right,' she continued steadily. 'You don't need to stop. Your body is shaking; just let that happen. It's all right to cry. It's all right to feel.'

She felt Stefano's eyes on her, knew she was talking as much to herself as to Lucio. *It's all right to feel. It was all right to hurt.*

She continued murmuring, affirming the emotions that ripped through his body and mind with exhausting force, until at last he sagged against his mother's shoulder, half-asleep. In that last moment before he lost consciousness, his eyes flickered open and he stared straight at Allegra.

'I saw,' he whispered, his voice scratchy and small. 'I saw and I ran away.'

Allegra stiffened in shock, even as Lucio relaxed into sleep. Bianca held him, stroking his hair, tears streaking silently down her face.

'You can keep holding him,' she told Bianca. 'For a while anyway, until he's fully asleep.'

'He spoke,' Bianca whispered, her eyes round and wide. 'He spoke. What did he say? Will he…will he be…?' She trailed off, unable to voice the hope they all cherished.

'It's a step in the right direction,' Allegra told her. 'That's good.'

She turned to the doorway, expecting to see Stefano, anticipating his smile of relief, but he was gone.

Allegra moved slowly down the hallway, aching in every part of her body, her mind. Her heart.

Lucio had, she hoped, just begun his journey of healing, and maybe—*maybe*—she had as well. She wanted—needed—to find Stefano and talk about what had happened.

He wasn't downstairs; the rooms were dark and empty. She looked in the art studio, saw only scattered brushes and broken glass.

After a moment's hesitation she turned and walked to the other end of the hallway and stood in front of his closed bedroom door. She knocked.

The soft sound seemed to reverberate through the emptiness in time with her own pounding heart. She knocked again.

After a long, laborious moment Stefano opened the door. Allegra's heart sank at the expression on his face. It was one she knew well; she knew it and hated it.

He smiled faintly, his eyes blank, everything about him distant and remote.

Don't touch me. Don't love me.

But she did, she realized, she did.

'Stefano?'

'Is Lucio all right?' he asked and she nodded.

'I know it's difficult to see, but releasing his suppressed emotion is definitely a step in the right direction.'

'It was a cathartic evening for everyone,' he agreed with that awful faint smile that spoke so clearly. *Don't come in. Don't get close.*

'Stefano…' He waited, eyebrows raised, one arm braced against the door-jamb, blocking her entry. 'May I come in?'

'I don't think that's a good idea.'

'Why are you shutting me out?' she asked, and heard the pain in her own voice. 'After I let you in. *I let you in.* Why?'

He smiled, and she saw a piercing gentleness in his eyes. He touched her cheek, let his fingers drift down her face and then fall away.

Away.

'You needed to tell someone everything that you'd been holding back,' he finally said. 'Like Lucio. But what happened afterwards—between us—was a mistake. Surely you see that. It didn't…' He paused, and she filled in the blanks.

'We were angry,' she said quietly. 'It wasn't right. I know that, but—'

Stefano shrugged his agreement. 'It's a good thing we stopped. That Lucio stopped us.'

'Why?' It hurt to ask, to be so vulnerable, so needy, but she wanted to know. She needed to know. 'Why?' she asked again. 'Stefano, I don't want us to be angry, but maybe we both need to finally address what is happening between us, what we *feel*—' She wanted to cry out, *I love you,* but she couldn't. Not yet, not when he was being so distant. She couldn't bear another silence, damning and endless.

She saw something like regret flicker across Stefano's features before he shook his head. 'Allegra, we agreed to put the past behind us, to be friends. So let's leave it at that.'

'Is that what you really want?'

Stefano was silent for a long moment, long enough for Allegra's fingers to curl into desperate claws, bunching against her legs, long enough for tears—yet more tears—to sting her eyes, to pool obviously, pathetically.

Long enough for him to realize how she felt, how she loved him, and still he didn't say anything.

And when he did finally speak, she wished he hadn't.

'Yes.' And, with that single devastating word, he gently—ever so gently—closed the door in her face.

On the other side of the door Stefano leaned against the wall and listened to Allegra's ragged breathing.

He'd hurt her. He knew that, and he was sorry.

So sorry, so damn *sorry,* but it was necessary.

He couldn't let her love him, not with all that hope and faith shining in her eyes, not when she was so willing to believe—again—that he could give her what she needed.

He couldn't. He knew he couldn't, and he was glad he knew, because now he wouldn't hurt her any more.

And he wouldn't hurt.

Nothing could be gained by their relationship, he knew, because he'd learned, finally, that he couldn't make her happy. He couldn't give her what she needed; his love was worthless and he'd only disappoint—devastate—her in the end.

And himself.

It was better this way, he told himself, even as he heard her choke back a sob of misery, even as he felt the answering howl in his own chest.

He closed his eyes, willed her to go before he opened the door and took her in his arms, kissed her and told her he didn't care if he couldn't make her happy, he wanted her anyway.

And he would have her.

Go.

Stefano's hand reached for the knob, curled slickly around it. He bit down hard on his lip, his eyes still clenched shut.

And then finally, slowly, he heard her retreat, the soft, disappointed patter of her footsteps down the hall.

Away.

Stefano pushed himself off the wall, sank on to his bed, one hand raking through his hair, hard enough to hurt.

Hurt.

It was better this way, he told himself, and tried desperately to believe it.

The next morning the sky was hard and bright, the sunshine pouring in the windows, bathing the room in light.

Allegra woke up from a disjointed, restless sleep, her hair tangled and sweaty against her face, her body aching as much as her heart was.

She hadn't realized until Stefano had closed the door in her face how much she'd counted on him to love her. Love her, she realized, as he always had. At nineteen, it hadn't been enough. She'd wanted more. She hadn't wanted the reality of love, its mess and complications. She'd wanted, as her mother had told her so cynically, the fairy tale.

But love wasn't a fairy tale. Love was hard, it was messy, it was painful and miserable and it made life worth living. For wrapped up in that pain, was unspeakable joy, unshakeable happiness, and she could have that with Stefano.

If he wanted it…

She felt her own hurt heart harden. He hadn't answered her seven years ago—*Do you love me?*—and he wouldn't answer now.

Why? *Why?*

Allegra sat up in bed and drew her knees up to her chest. She'd believed for so long that Stefano hadn't loved her. It had become the bedrock of her soul, of her outlook. She'd clung to it because it justified her own actions, her own feelings.

She'd seen him tender, terrible, and everything in between, all the emotions in a tangle, just like hers were.

She loved him, and she'd fought it with every ounce of her being. What if Stefano was the same way?

What if he loved her and didn't want to? Was afraid to, even?

What if he felt just like she did?

The thought was quite literally incredible, yet it was also wondrous and frightening.

If Stefano loved her…then all she needed to do was make him admit it. Confess.

An impossible task.

Allegra shook her head. She couldn't think about Stefano, couldn't let her thoughts get in such a hopeless tangle. She needed to concentrate on Lucio and his recovery. And, to do that, she needed help.

She showered and dressed quickly before heading downstairs for breakfast. Bianca was in the kitchen and Lucio was at the table eating breakfast.

'Hello, Bianca,' Allegra greeted the housekeeper. Bianca had shadows of fatigue under her eyes but she looked happy. Relieved. 'Hello, Lucio,' she said, crouching down to meet Lucio's reluctant gaze, one hand steady and firm on his shoulder.

He was silent for a long moment, his gaze sliding away from hers, but Allegra waited. Finally he jerked his head in a greeting and whispered, 'Hello.'

Bianca beamed; Allegra smiled. 'Would you like to do art with me today?'

Another jerking nod. Allegra accepted it; it was enough. She sat down to breakfast.

Stefano didn't appear as she ate, and she didn't need Bianca to tell her that he'd returned to Rome.

He was the one running away now, she thought with a sad smile. When would he return? And what would she say? Do?

After breakfast she took Lucio up to the art studio. Thankfully, someone had cleaned up the broken glass and brushes, and Allegra wondered who it was. Bianca, being polite? Or Stefano, trying to forget what had happened between them...deny that it ever had?

'Why don't you take a look around, Lucio?' she suggested. 'Would you like to draw something? Paint? We could take the clay out.'

Lucio went tentatively to the crayons. He selected a green one and began, ever so carefully, to draw grass. A field.

Allegra watched silently as his picture, and his memory, slowly took shape. A field, a red box with black circles on one side—a tractor, Allegra realized, overturned.

And, behind a rock, a stick figure. A boy, with oversized tears, big black drops, falling from his circle of a face.

After a long moment Lucio thrust the picture at her. His face was hard, determined.

'Is this what you saw, Lucio?' Allegra asked gently. 'You saw your father in the tractor?'

His lip trembled and his eyes filled as he nodded. 'I should have been in bed...I wanted to see Papa... He looked over at me and waved...' He stopped talking, started to shake.

Allegra put a hand on his shoulder. She could guess the rest. Enzo, while waving to his son, had taken his eyes from the field, hit a rock or tree stump, and the tractor had overturned. Lucio had seen the whole thing and, terrified, had run away.

I ran away.

'Lucio, thank you for telling me. I know that was a hard thing to do. It's hard to tell the truth. But it's not your fault that your papa died, even if you feel it is. It's not your fault.'

Lucio gulped back a sob, shook his head. 'I ran away.'

'You were scared. You didn't know what to do. It's not your fault.' Allegra spoke gently, firmly, but Lucio just shook his head, unable to believe, to accept the absolution Allegra offered him.

'I want Mama,' he whispered and after a moment Allegra nodded.

'Let's go find your mama,' she said, slipping his hand into hers and leading him from the room, from the pain of his memories.

Later, when Lucio was sleeping, she spoke to Bianca and explained what had happened.

'And he saw…?' Bianca's face was pale, horrified. 'My poor Lucio! And all this time he's held it in?'

'He feels guilty,' Allegra explained. 'Guilty for being there in the first place, and then for running away. He'll need to talk to a psychiatrist, Bianca. He'll need therapy, more than I can provide, to process and accept what has happened.'

Bianca nodded. 'But do you think…in time…?' she whispered.

'The more support he's given, the better chance there is of Lucio accepting what has happened and moving on,' Allegra said, trying to keep her voice encouraging even as she felt mired by doubts.

Did anyone have a chance of accepting the mistakes and tragedies of the past and moving on? Living, loving again?

'I hope so,' she said with a watery smile. 'I pray so.'

Bianca nodded fervently. 'So do I.'

They sat in silence for a moment, the shadows lengthening, the mountains wrapped in the soft violet light of dusk.

'I'd like to go to Milan,' Allegra said after a moment, 'and talk to Dr Speri. He's a gifted psychiatrist, and he'll have some recommendations for Lucio, what course of action to take next.'

Bianca nodded. 'Whatever you must do.'

Allegra tried to keep her voice diffident as she asked, 'Do you know when Stefano will be back?'

'He didn't say.' Bianca smiled sadly. 'He looked terrible this morning, as if he hadn't slept at all.'

Allegra nodded. 'I didn't sleep much, either,' she admitted.

'What is happening? You're in love, *si?*'

Allegra was silent for a long moment. Yes, they were in love. She believed—she had to believe—that Stefano loved her. Finally she shrugged, her smile one of sorrow and regret. 'Sometimes,' she said, 'love isn't enough.'

'Love is always enough,' Bianca protested, and Allegra wished it could be true. Yet it hadn't been true seven years ago. Love hadn't been enough then, not nearly enough.

She knew, in her heart, she'd been right to run. Even though she loved him now, she could never have made Stefano happy then, and he would have made her miserable.

Funny, she thought without any humour, when she felt that he could make her very happy now, if he'd let himself. And she could make him happy—she hoped—if he let her in.

She left the next morning for Milan. Bianca drove her to the train station in L'Aquila, Lucio sitting in the back seat. It was the first time he'd been away from the environs of the villa in months, and Allegra was glad that he seemed to accept it.

The train journey took a few hours—hours which she spent leaning her head against the window, watching the barren mountains and empty fields turn to hill towns and prosperous suburbs, and then finally the busy, glittering metropolis of Milan.

She'd rung Dr Speri the previous afternoon and he'd agreed to spare her an hour to talk about Lucio.

Sitting in his office, she explained the situation, the progress Lucio had made.

'The poor boy,' Dr Speri said after she'd spoken. 'To suffer so much, and so silently.'

'I feel out of my depth,' Allegra confessed frankly. 'He needs more intensive therapy than I can provide.'

'You've done wonders, Allegra, as you did before,' Dr Speri said with a smile. 'I'm impressed.'

Allegra gave a short laugh. 'It isn't me, Dr Speri. It's the children. They reach a point where they're willing to confront their emotions and memories, and I happen to be there.'

'I think it's a bit more than that.'

Allegra smiled, but secretly she wondered if it really was. How had she been able to help children like Lucio when she'd hidden from her own self for so long?

Yet now that was going to change. She wasn't going to run away, she wasn't going to hide. She would face the truth and she would make a future.

There had been another reason to come to Milan.

After leaving Dr Speri with several recommendations for local child psychiatrists, she took a taxi to a quiet neighbourhood of tall, elegant town houses. Minutes from the fashionable Via Montenapoleone, the neighbourhood reeked sophistication and snobbery.

It was where her mother lived.

Allegra pressed the doorbell with a shaking but determined finger. She didn't know if her mother would be home; she didn't know if she wanted her to be.

After a moment she heard footsteps and wondered who would actually open the door: a harassed maid, a scantily clad lover, or her mother herself?

It was the last, looking older and harder than she had seven years ago. She was more polished, more brittle, her hair expertly highlighted to a platinum blonde, her face Botoxed, her nails long, false, and painted a glossy hot pink.

Her thin red lips curved in a knowing, mocking smile. 'Well, well,' she said. 'The prodigal daughter returns.'

'Hello, Mama,' Allegra said. 'May I come in?'

'By all means.' Her mother threw an arm out in a wide, expansive arc, ushering Allegra into her home.

Allegra moved into a drawing room that was elegant, impersonal and cold. She stood in the middle of the room while her mother sprawled on to a white leather divan.

'Go on, make yourself comfortable,' she said with a little laugh. Allegra perched on the edge of a spindly antique chair.

'I came,' she said after a moment, watching as her mother lit a cigarette and blew a long thin stream of smoke in the air, 'because I wanted to make peace with you.'

Her mother took another drag on her cigarette. 'How very touching.'

'I've been angry at you, you and Papa both, for a long time. I didn't even realize how angry or hurt I really was until recently, and I want to make it right.'

Her mother's thin, perfectly plucked eyebrows rose in disbelieving arcs. 'It must be very convenient,' she said dryly, 'to blame other people for your own mistakes.'

Allegra stared at her. 'What do you mean?'

'You aren't seriously telling me,' her mother continued, 'that you've blamed me for walking out on your poor fiancé all those years ago? You aren't, surely, going to lay all that at my door?' Her smile was so vicious that Allegra felt as if she'd been assaulted.

'No, of course not,' she said after a moment. 'I take responsibility for what I did. I chose to leave, even if you gave me a push in that direction. I almost turned back—'

'But you didn't, and you shouldn't have,' Isabel cut in. 'Allegra, you thought Stefano was your knight in shining armour. When you realized he wasn't, you deserted him. It's really that simple.'

Allegra's mouth dropped open. It was so close to what Stefano had intimated before, and yet it was wrong. *Wrong*. 'It wasn't that simple,' she said, fighting to keep her voice steady. 'The marriage was arranged and no one told me!'

'Oh, really? And you just thought Stefano appeared at your party by magic? And wanted to dance with you, be with you—you, a pathetic little frump of a child?'

Allegra forced herself to meet her mother's scathing gaze. Kept her chin held high, even though it hurt.

It hurt.

'Yes, I did,' she said. 'I realize now just how innocent—ignorant—I truly was, but I believed, and no one told me otherwise.'

'And why should we?' Isabel demanded. 'Stefano was attentive to you, kind and considerate. He might not have loved you—how could he have?—but that could have come in time.'

'Then why didn't you tell me that at the time?' Allegra demanded, her voice shaking, her composure starting to crack.

'I did,' Isabel replied succinctly, 'but it wasn't enough for you.'

'You urged me to leave,' Allegra said in a low voice. 'You told me you would have left yourself—'

'And I would have,' Isabel replied. 'I did, in the end. But your father was a very different man from Stefano. Cruel, callous and utterly unfaithful.'

'You said Stefano would be the same! That I'd be glad, in the end, if he turned to other women—'

'I was speaking from experience,' Isabel said in a bored voice. 'And what does it matter? You chose for yourself, Allegra. You chose to listen to me. Accept it.'

'Stefano treated me like a possession, a child—'

'You were a child,' Isabel said with a laugh. 'How else was he supposed to treat you?'

Allegra shook her head. 'No. It wouldn't have worked. We wouldn't have worked.' She couldn't believe that it had all been a mistake. She wouldn't. 'You might have used the situation to your own advantage to shame Papa, but I know I was right.'

'I'm so thrilled for you,' Isabel stated dryly.

Allegra lifted her eyes to meet her mother's hard, unflinching gaze. 'Why?' she asked. 'Why did you want to shame him so much?'

'Because he shamed me every day of our marriage,' Isabel snapped, and there was a savage edge of pain to her voice that Allegra had never heard before, a sound that made her sad. 'And shame him I did,' she added, gloating now. 'In front of five hundred people, sweating in his suit, humiliated beyond endurance! It was a beautiful moment.'

Allegra watched her mother smile in twisted, triumphant memory, felt the words—the realization—penetrate.

'What are you talking about?' she whispered. 'I told you—you said—you'd give my note to Stefano before the ceremony! So he wouldn't be shamed—'

Isabel shrugged. 'I changed my mind.'

'What! Are you telling me that Stefano went to the church thinking I would be there? That he *waited?*'

Isabel smiled, cruel enjoyment dancing in her eyes. 'As your father did. I didn't care about Stefano, although you obviously did. But yes, he stood there. He waited.' She laughed. 'And all of his peasant relatives waited too! I knew Stefano had money, but his family obviously grew up on a pig farm. His mother had about three teeth, dressed all in black. She looked like the worst kind of drudge.'

'Don't talk about them like that!' Allegra's voice rose in a sharp cry. She thought of the men in the village, kissing her, bestowing their blessings.

They'd been there, she realized with a sickening wave of understanding. They'd all stood by Stefano—Bianca too—and had watched him wait.

Had watched him be shamed.

She imagined the prissy shock and gloating malice of her family's snobbish friends, pictured Stefano standing still and straight as the minutes ticked by and no bride came. She wondered when he'd realized she wasn't coming, when he'd finally walked out of the church and five hundred staring guests.

The only thing that was hurt that day was your pride.

And how hurt it was! She'd never known, never realized…

'Don't tell me you didn't know that,' Isabel said in disbelief. 'How could you not have heard? George would have told you, or Daphne—'

'No.' Allegra shook her head. She hadn't let anyone speak of the wedding; she hadn't wanted to hear. 'No.'

'Then you really did stick your head in the sand,' Isabel said with an almost admiring laugh. 'Well, let me pull it out for you. Yes, he waited. He waited for hours. Even after the guests had gone, after his family told him to leave. Your father had already started drinking, demanding money, calling in his debts.' Isabel shook her head. 'If I'd realized how thinly he'd spread himself—I didn't get one euro out of it!'

'Papa *shot* himself,' Allegra said, her voice trembling, tears starting to fall.

'Yes, I know. I was there, remember? You weren't.' Isabel shrugged, unmoved. 'In the end, he was a pathetic waste of man.'

'As you are a waste of a mother! How could you do that to Stefano? To me?'

'Why do you care now?' Isabel asked coolly. 'You were perfectly content to shame him in leaving him, Allegra. Leaving him with nothing but a note—a note you couldn't even write yourself! Not one word of explanation or understanding. And yet you blame me.'

'I never wanted to hurt him,' Allegra whispered.

'Yes, you did.' Isabel's voice was forceful, violent. 'You might not want to admit it, even to yourself, not then and not now, but you did. You wanted to hurt him as he'd hurt you— treating you like a child, telling you he didn't love you. So you did it the only way you knew how—the coward's way. And I, being the gracious mother I am, helped.' Isabel's teeth were bared in a horrible smile.

Allegra shrank back. 'No.' And yet, no matter how coldly or cruelly her mother phrased it, she heard the truth. She knew it, recognised it even after seven years of self-righteous blame and denial.

She'd wanted to hurt Stefano, even to shame him. Hadn't cared about the consequences, hadn't wanted to know.

And now they were staring her down, crowding her out. Memories. Feelings. Regrets.

No wonder Stefano was angry, she thought hollowly. No wonder he pushed her away, told her he didn't want her any more. No wonder he didn't want to love her.

Why would he? Why would he, when she'd treated him so terribly? Who would sign up for that kind of love, that kind of life, again?

But he hurt me.

Yes, he'd hurt her and she needed to forgive him. And he, Allegra realized, needed to forgive her.

Only then could they go forward. Only then could love—wonderful, painful, messy love—be enough.

'Thank you,' she told her mother stiffly, 'for enlightening me so thoroughly.' She'd come here for closure and instead had the past ripped open all the more. Yet she'd needed to know. She'd hidden from the truth of her own heart for so long; she wouldn't hide from the truth of her actions. 'I won't be seeing you again.'

Isabel waved a hand with languid indifference. 'Fine.'

Allegra walked on legs that felt wooden to the door of the drawing room, then turned around. 'I feel sorry for you,' she stated in a calm, cool voice.

Isabel stared at her, nonplussed, and Allegra shook her head. 'You can't be happy.'

For a moment Isabel's face was naked in its desolate emotion, the unassailable loneliness of her life and the choices she had made. Then her cold composure returned, and she shrugged with defiant indifference.

'Goodbye, Mama,' Allegra said quietly, and left the town house.

All the way back to L'Aquila, her thoughts sifted and seethed. Truth, memory, hurt, forgiveness.

They'd both tried to forget the past and pretend it didn't matter. But they couldn't; no one could.

The past wasn't forgotten until it was forgiven.

Forgiveness—forgiveness and being forgiven—was hard. It was messy and painful, just like love.

She closed her eyes, dreading and desiring the confrontation ahead, the reckoning that had needed to come since she'd met Stefano in the hotel foyer—no, since she'd left him one moonlit night.

It would come now. She would make it so.

Allegra took a taxi from L'Aquila back to the villa. As the old car wound its way up the twisted roads, past the half-deserted hill towns, she realized that it felt like coming home.

Home. Home was where Stefano was, and who knew when he would be back?

Yet she would wait and, if necessary, she would find him. She would do whatever it took to confront the past. To heal it.

Bianca greeted her with a warm embrace when the taxi pulled up at the villa and even Lucio came and touched her hand, smiling shyly.

Over coffee in the kitchen, Allegra explained what Dr Speri had told her.

'There is support available locally,' she said. 'He gave me the names of therapists and psychiatrists in L'Aquila, as well as grief counselling for both of you.' She smiled and squeezed Bianca's hand. 'It won't be easy, but it will be better. It will help.'

Bianca nodded. 'I never expected it to be easy,' she said. 'I am just glad that finally we can do something. Thank you.'

Allegra smiled and nodded her acceptance. She watched Lucio playing on the floor, his face still fixed in concentration, and knew it wouldn't be easy or simple.

Nothing was. Love wasn't.

'Have you heard from Stefano?' she asked, and Bianca heard the intensity in her voice and smiled sadly.

'No, but he will come back. He will have to.'

Allegra nodded, knowing that Bianca spoke with the unshakeable conviction that Stefano loved her. Yet still she wasn't so sure.

She wanted to be sure, wanted to believe, to hope, but how could she, when he'd left her without a word?

Not even a note.

Yet what she was sure of—finally, futilely, perhaps—was that she loved Stefano.

And she would tell him so.

Yet, as the days passed, the wind sharpening, the leaves beginning to flutter disconsolately from the trees, Allegra wondered if she would be given the opportunity.

Stefano had not rung, hadn't written. Hadn't come home.

She had no idea where he was, what he was doing, what he thought.

She'd spent the days with Lucio, continuing his therapy as well as travelling to L'Aquila to work with the new grief counsellor he and Bianca would be meeting together.

Lucio spoke now—few, halting words, his face still sometimes lost in shadow, transfixed by tragedy—and Allegra knew it would take a lot of time and a lot of healing before he could move on.

But she was optimistic, determined, and so was Bianca.

A week after her trip to Milan, Allegra decided to leave again. Lucio needed her less, as he was regularly meeting a psychiatrist and grief counsellor, as well as starting up again with his nursery school.

Although she didn't like to leave the villa and Lucio, she knew he could tolerate her absence for a few days…enough time to find Stefano.

She'd start with his flat in Rome, she decided. It was one of two links she had, as he'd also given her his email address.

Laying her suitcase on her bed, she began to pack for a trip that would end where? And with what?

She had no idea, only hope and the sure knowledge of her own feelings at last.

Her suitcase was half-packed and she was sorting through a few clothes when she heard her door swing open, heard the sudden, hostile hiss of indrawn breath, and before she could even turn, words of bitter condemnation, utter judgement.

'So,' Stefano said, 'you're running away again.'

CHAPTER TEN

ALLEGRA WHIRLED AROUND, shock turning her rigid. 'Stefano!'

His face was twisted with rage, with bitterness, with pain. Hurt.

'Running away,' he spat, 'without even telling me where you're going or why. I should have expected it. I've been waiting for it.'

It took Allegra's mind a moment to catch up, to realize what Stefano had assumed simply from a half-packed bag. When she realized his mistake, relief poured through, sweet and exhilarating. She almost laughed. 'Stefano, no, no, this isn't—'

'Why, Allegra?' His voice was ragged. 'Why, after all this time, can you not spare the decency of an explanation? A conversation, face to face? What are you scared of?' His voice rose on both a plea and an accusation. 'Or do you just not care?'

'I do care,' Allegra whispered. 'I do.'

'You have a bizarre way of showing it,' Stefano said. He turned away, jerking his shoulder in a shrug. 'Go, then. Go and don't come back.' And with that he strode from her room, slamming the door, leaving her alone and stunned.

She took a few calming breaths. This went deeper, required more than a simple sentence of explanation. A lot more.

It took Allegra a few seconds to gather her courage, her conviction, but when she did she was unshakeable. She stormed from the room, stalked down the hall and met him in his bedroom.

He stood by the window, head bowed in defeat, fingers fisted in his hair, and Allegra's heart ached. Broke.

Her self-righteous indignation trickled away as she knew it should have done long ago.

'Stefano, I'm not going anywhere,' she said quietly. He didn't answer, didn't even turn. 'I was…' she continued, 'I was planning on going to Rome—to find you. To tell you—'

'It doesn't matter,' he said. When he looked up, his face was blank, his voice cold. 'To tell you the truth, Allegra, I really don't care.' He turned from the window and moved past her with supreme indifference. He stood by the door and Allegra realized he was waiting for her to leave. Her mouth opened in shock.

'You do care!' she cried. 'You just showed me you cared!'

'I was disappointed,' Stefano corrected with cold disdain, 'for Lucio's sake. I thought you cared more about him and your own work—'

'No, Stefano. This is not about Lucio. It's about us. *Us*.' Allegra's voice shook. 'You don't care just for Lucio. You care about yourself. You care about me. And I'm beginning to realize that you always did.'

Stefano was silent for a long, terrible moment. Allegra stood her ground, waiting for him to look at her. When he did, her heart lurched at the sardonic gleam in his amber eyes.

'Oh?' Stefano queried softly. He raised one eyebrow. 'But I treated you like a possession, Allegra, remember? Like an *object*. You told me so yourself, you found me out.' He moved towards her with lithe, lethal grace and, although she trembled, Allegra didn't move. She would stand her ground this time, no matter what.

She wouldn't run away.

'What's made you think I care about you, Allegra?' he asked when he was just a whisper away. He reached out and touched her cheek, let his hand drift with mocking knowledge to her breast.

Allegra trembled, but she didn't move. His eyes blazed into

hers and he pulled his hand away with a sound of disgust. 'Or are you simply so desperate, so pathetic, that you've managed to convince yourself despite the evidence otherwise?'

Allegra's face flamed, then paled. She felt her fingers curl into slick fists. 'You're saying these things,' she said steadily, 'because you're angry.'

'Angry?' Stefano sounded incredulous. 'Why should I be angry? From what I hear, you've made wonderful progress with Lucio. You've done everything I asked.'

'Stefano, this isn't about Lucio!' Allegra's voice rose in a frustrated shout. She strove to calm herself, to reach him when he was trying so hard to be remote, removed. 'I told you, it's about us. And yes, you're angry. I saw it that first evening, at Daphne's reception. It was in your eyes.'

Stefano folded his arms. 'This all sounds very melodramatic,' he commented in a bored drawl.

'I felt it,' Allegra continued, 'the night after the party in Rome. The way you touched me—'

'Like a possession,' Stefano cut her off swiftly. 'As you accused me. Well, it's true, isn't it? Everything you've said is true.' His voice rang with condemnation—condemnation of himself as well as her—and it shamed Allegra. She'd believed the worst of him…always.

Except now.

'Stefano, please. Listen to me. I spoke to my mother today—'

'Cosy times,' Stefano drawled and she closed her eyes, praying for patience. She had so much to say, to ask, and it was impossible when he was like this, cutting her off before she could even begin to get close.

Because he didn't want her to get close. He didn't want to get hurt…again.

It was such a strange and humbling thought, to consider that Stefano had been hurt—truly, deeply wounded—by her actions all those years ago. And for that she had to ask his forgiveness…if he would even let her. If he would admit to being hurt, which she was beginning to doubt he would. *Could.*

'My mother told me,' Allegra tried again, forcing her voice not to waver, 'that you waited at the church for me, all those years ago.'

He gave a short laugh of disbelief. 'Of course I did, Allegra. We were getting married, remember? We'd actually agreed to meet there, funnily enough.' His eyes were hard, his mouth flattening into a thin line of anger and disgust.

'Would you believe,' Allegra asked, 'that I didn't know? That I asked her to give you my letter the evening before? I didn't want you to be humiliated in front of everyone.'

He stared at her for a long, hard moment, his eyes raking over her in judgement. 'I don't know why we're talking about this now. It doesn't matter.'

'You're right,' Allegra agreed. 'It doesn't matter that I wanted to give you the note the night before, because I still ran away. I left everyone else to deal with my mess because I was young and afraid. And selfish,' she added. 'I was selfish. When I heard you talking with my father, and then with me, it was as if you were a different man—one I was almost afraid of. And when you didn't answer me when I asked you if you loved me, I assumed you didn't.' She paused, her throat aching with the effort of this confession, spoken to a stone wall of indifference. Stefano gazed at her, arms still folded, a bored look on his face.

Why did this have to be so hard? Why couldn't he *say* something?

Yet she knew somehow that this was right, this was fitting. She'd faced his silence before and she'd run away. She'd been too afraid, too young, too silly to voice all the fears and needs in her heart, and now she would.

Now she would say everything.

'I should have told you what I was feeling,' Allegra continued. 'But I was a child, Stefano, as you knew I was. And I loved you like a child. You were right: when I saw you weren't my

perfect prince, I ran away. I couldn't face it and I ran away.'
He gave a little shrug, unmoved, and she took a breath. 'But
now I'm a woman, and I love you like a woman, and I'm not
running away.'

Something flickered across his face. His mouth twisted and
his shoulder jerked and then he spun away, stalked to the
window. Allegra watched as he braced one arm against the
window frame, his body taut with suppressed tension.

'Stefano…'

'Once upon a time,' he said in a harsh voice, 'I would have
given much—anything—to hear you say that. But not now.
Not now.'

'I know,' Allegra said after a moment, her voice trembling,
'that I need to ask you to forgive me. I know why you've been
angry, and you have a right to be, Stefano. When I think of you
standing there, waiting for me, and all your family, your mother,
the men from the village there—' She broke off, tears starting
and then streaming down her face. 'I'm sorry,' she whispered.
'I'm so sorry. Will you forgive me?'

Stefano's back was still to her. He straightened, raking one
hand through his hair before dropping it lifelessly to his side.
Slowly, sorrowfully, he shook his head. 'You're right, I have been
angry. Like you, I fought my emotions. My memories. I'd convinced myself I didn't feel anything for you, never did. I almost
believed that all I'd ever really wanted from you was your name.'

Allegra held her breath, waited.

'I almost succeeded,' Stefano continued, his back to her as
he gazed out of the window at the deepening twilight. 'I married
Gabriella and I thought I could manage it. But she made me miserable, as I told you, and I did the same to her. It was bitter then
to realize what a mistake I'd made, what a fool I'd been. I'd ex-
changed something I'd believed to be deep and real for something shallow and false. I didn't want a marriage simply for a
name. I didn't want a *possession*. I wanted you. I wanted love.'

Allegra opened her mouth, made a tiny breath of sound, but

realized she didn't know what to say. Stefano must have heard her too, for he continued.

'But it wasn't deep or real, was it? Because it fell apart at the first gate.'

Allegra wanted to deny it, yet she knew she couldn't. Every word Stefano spoke was true, terribly true. Their love hadn't survived the first test, and she knew it never would have survived a marriage. She'd been too young, too idealistic and impressionable. And Stefano? Stefano had had his own weaknesses, his own faults—ones that he was acknowledging now.

If only, Allegra thought, he could believe they were different now. Stronger.

'I know you believed I didn't love you,' Stefano said into the silence. 'And that I thought of you as an object. And I know now that my love was flawed. Perhaps, in some ways, I did think of you the way you believed I did. It's hard to remember now. Yet, when I saw you again, I wasn't prepared to feel anything. I still managed to keep convincing myself that I never felt anything for you, and then to see you…and want you…and know that, even though you desired me, you also reviled me.'

'I didn't—'

Stefano shrugged. 'It's unimportant now.' He straightened, and she wished she could see his face. She wanted to look into his eyes and see *something* there.

'So yes, I forgive you, Allegra,' Stefano said, 'since you seem to need to hear that. I forgave you a long time ago. I know you were young and frightened, influenced by your mother. *Da tutti i san,* I'm not a monster. I wasn't then, though I know you thought me one.'

'I didn't—' Allegra tried again, but stopped as Stefano half-turned to her.

In the lengthening shadows she saw him smile sadly. 'The way you looked at me? I knew, Allegra. I knew every thought in your head. I knew you realized I wasn't your dashing prince, and I knew you questioned what kind of man I was. Why ask me if I loved you, if you were sure?'

'*Did* you love me?' Allegra whispered and he laughed, a broken, empty sound.

'Even now you don't know? Even now you have to ask?' He turned around, spread his hands wide, his head thrown back. 'But of course you do. Because the kind of man I am, the kind of love I offer is *worthless* to you! Well, I know it. You've told me time and time again. You don't want what I have to give, Allegra. It's never enough for you. I saw that seven years ago. I realized it when you asked me those questions, when you looked at me as if somehow I could make it all right again. And I knew I couldn't. I never could.' His voice was ragged, his eyes bleak with a despairing knowledge. 'And I can't give it to you now. You've shown me, you've told me. Even moments ago…' He broke off and rubbed a hand over his face. 'I came back from Rome to tell you I loved you, and you seemed to have already guessed it, but it doesn't matter. It doesn't matter. So why are we putting ourselves through this? We won't work, Allegra. Love isn't enough.'

It was what she had said to Bianca, what she'd believed, yet now she knew it wasn't true. Knew it with her heart, soul, body and mind.

Love was enough.

'Love is enough, Stefano,' she said, 'when it comes with honesty, like we're being now, and with forgiveness. And all the other things you can give me, that you've already given me. You showed me how you love when you took me in your arms and wiped away my tears. And before then—when you look at Lucio. When you embraced those men. When you spoke about your family. Stefano!' Her voice rang out clear and strong. 'Your love is enough.'

He began to shake his head, but she stopped him. She crossed to him, certain now, her doubts and fears falling away in the light of the one simple truth that made all the difference:

they loved each other. She knew it now, saw it in Stefano's eyes, felt it in her own soul.

They loved each other, and it was enough.

It would be.

She stood in front of him, stood on tiptoe to cup his face in her hands. She felt the stubble on his cheeks, glinting gold in the settling dusk, and felt with her thumbs a dampness near his eyes.

'The only question I have to ask now is this,' she said softly. 'Is my love enough for you?'

Stefano gave a small, choked cry of assent, then reached up to press her hand against his cheek. Allegra blinked back tears as he dropped his hand to pull her into a closer, deeper embrace.

'Yes,' he whispered. '*Yes.*'

She'd never felt so comforted, so safe—so protected, so provided for—than she did in the shelter of Stefano's arms.

They stood that way for a long time, silent, still, and utterly content, as twilight settled softly over the villa, cloaking the distant peaks in a soft purple light that brought peace to the world.

Everything was different this time. Allegra stood in the vestibule of the tiny church and smiled at her reflection. Instead of ruffles and lace, she wore a simple silk sheath in palest ivory. Her hair was down, tumbling over her shoulders in a cascade of sunlight, and diamond teardrop earrings sparkled at her ears.

She felt a small hand tug on her dress and she looked down and smiled at Lucio. He smiled back shyly and ducked his head.

Lucio had been in therapy for three months and he was doing much better. The strides were slow but they were there, and Allegra was thankful.

She was thankful for so much.

There were only a handful of people in the church for the ceremony. No glittering names or faces, just a few friends from the village, Bianca and Lucio, and another couple of people from London. Neither of them wanted a spectacle.

They wanted a ceremony—simple, sacred.

It was enough.

'Are you ready?' Bianca's father, Matteo, stooped and in a wrinkled suit that smelled faintly of mothballs, stood by Allegra's elbow.

'Yes,' she said, and took his arm.

The organ played music, but Allegra barely heard it as she walked down the narrow aisle of cracked stone. Stefano stood at the end of it, dressed immaculately in a charcoal grey suit, his hands folded at his front, love blazing from his eyes.

Allegra's heart swelled and she almost stumbled, still, after all this time, not used to heels.

Matteo steadied her and she walked firmly the rest of the way to stand proudly by Stefano's side.

Both of their voices rang out with clear purpose as they said their vows.

'*Noi promettiamo di amarci fedelmente, nella gioia e nel dolore, nella salute e nella malattia, e di sostenerci l'un l'altro tutti i giorni della nostra vita...*'

We promise to love each other faithfully, in the joy and the pain, the health and the disease, and to every day support each other in our life.

Allegra knew they both meant it, every word.

They had a wedding supper at the villa, and then Bianca left with Lucio to spend the night at her father's. Stefano had wanted to take her to a hotel, somewhere luxurious and opulent, but Allegra simply wanted this—to be home, *home,* with him.

She stood by the window where they'd found each other at last just over three months ago and watched as darkness crept over the mountains. She'd never tire of the view, she thought, watching as the first stars twinkled on the jagged horizon.

Stefano came to stand beside her, his hands on her shoulders. He bent to kiss the nape of her neck, and Allegra shivered with pleasure.

She turned to face him and he kissed her, deeply, with a passion that was tender and yet powerful in its force.

She looked up at him, into his eyes, saw the light of his love shining there. There were no shadows, no flickers, no doubts, no fears. No anger.

'Come,' Stefano said, lacing his fingers with hers, and with gentle purpose he led her to their marriage bed.

* * * * *

Harlequin is 60 years old,
and Harlequin Blaze is celebrating!
After all, a lot can happen in 60 years,
or 60 minutes…or 60 seconds!
Find out what's going down in Blaze's
heart-stopping new mini-series,
FROM 0 TO 60!
Getting from "Hello" to "How was it?"
can happen fast….

Here's a sneak peek of the first book,
A LONG HARD RIDE
by Alison Kent
Available March 2009

"Is that for me?" Trey asked.

Cardin Worth cocked her head to the side and considered how much better the day already seemed. "Good morning to you, too."

When she didn't hold out the second cup of coffee for him to take, he came closer. She sipped from her heavy white mug, hiding her grin and her giddy rush of nerves behind it.

But when he stopped in front of her, she made the mistake of lowering her gaze from his face to the exposed strip of his chest. It was either give him his cup of coffee or bury her nose against him and breathe in. She remembered so clearly how he smelled. How he tasted.

She gave him his coffee.

After taking a quick gulp, he smiled and said, "Good morning, Cardin. I hope the floor wasn't too hard for you."

The hardness of the floor hadn't been the problem. She shook her head. "Are you kidding? I slept like a baby, swaddled in my sleeping bag."

"In my sleeping bag, you mean."

If he wanted to get technical, yeah. "Thanks for the loaner. It made sleeping on the floor almost bearable." As had the warmth of his spooned body, she thought, then quickly changed the subject. "I saw you have a loaf of bread and some eggs. Would you like me to cook breakfast?"

He lowered his coffee mug slowly, his gaze as warm as the

sun on her shoulders, as the ceramic heating her hands. "I didn't bring you out here to wait on me."

"You didn't bring me out here at all. I volunteered to come."

"To help me get ready for the race. Not to serve me."

"It's just breakfast, Trey. And coffee." Even if last night it had been more. Even if the way he was looking at her made her want to climb back into that sleeping bag. "I work much better when my stomach's not growling. I thought it might be the same for you."

"It is, but I'll cook. You made the coffee."

"That's because I can't work at all without caffeine."

"If I'd known that, I would've put on a pot as soon I got up."

"What time *did* you get up?" Judging by the sun's position, she swore it couldn't be any later than seven now. And, yeah, they'd agreed to start working at six.

"Maybe four?" he guessed, giving her a lazy smile.

"But it was almost two…" She let the sentence dangle, finishing the thought privately. She was quite sure he knew exactly what time they'd finally fallen asleep after he'd made love to her.

The question facing her now was where did this relationship—if you could even call it *that*—go from here?

* * * * *

*Cardin and Trey are about to find out that
great sex is only the beginning….
Don't miss the fireworks!
Get ready for
A LONG HARD RIDE
by Alison Kent
Available March 2009,
wherever Blaze books are sold.*

HARLEQUIN *Presents*

International Billionaires

Life is a game of power and pleasure.
And these men play to win!

AT THE ARGENTINIAN BILLIONAIRE'S BIDDING
by *India Grey*

Billionaire Alejandro D'Arienzo desires revenge
on Tamsin—the heiress who wrecked his past.
Tamsin is shocked when Alejandro threatens her
business with his ultimatum: *her name in tatters
or her body in his bed...*
Book #2806

Available March 2009

Eight volumes in all to collect!

REQUEST YOUR FREE BOOKS!

2 FREE NOVELS PLUS 2
FREE GIFTS!

PASSION
GUARANTEED
SEDUCTION

YES! Please send me 2 FREE Harlequin Presents® novels and my 2 FREE gifts (gifts are worth about $10). After receiving them, if I don't wish to receive any more books, I can return the shipping statement marked "cancel". If I don't cancel, I will receive 6 brand-new novels every month and be billed just $4.05 per book in the U.S. or $4.74 per book in Canada, plus 25¢ shipping and handling per book and applicable taxes, if any*. That's a savings of close to 15% off the cover price! I understand that accepting the 2 free books and gifts places me under no obligation to buy anything. I can always return a shipment and cancel at any time. Even if I never buy another book, the two free books and gifts are mine to keep forever.   106 HDN ERRW   306 HDN ERRL

Name _____ (PLEASE PRINT) _____

Address _____ Apt. # _____

City _____ State/Prov. _____ Zip/Postal Code _____

Signature (if under 18, a parent or guardian must sign)

Mail to the **Harlequin Reader Service:**
IN U.S.A.: P.O. Box 1867, Buffalo, NY 14240-1867
IN CANADA: P.O. Box 609, Fort Erie, Ontario L2A 5X3

Not valid to current subscribers of Harlequin Presents books.

Want to try two free books from another line?
Call 1-800-873-8635 or visit www.morefreebooks.com.

* Terms and prices subject to change without notice. N.Y. residents add applicable sales tax. Canadian residents will be charged applicable provincial taxes and GST. Offer not valid in Quebec. This offer is limited to one order per household. All orders subject to approval. Credit or debit balances in a customer's account(s) may be offset by any other outstanding balance owed by or to the customer. Please allow 4 to 6 weeks for delivery. Offer available while quantities last.

Your Privacy: Harlequin Books is committed to protecting your privacy. Our Privacy Policy is available online at www.eHarlequin.com or upon request from the Reader Service. From time to time we make our lists of customers available to reputable third parties who may have a product or service of interest to you. If you would prefer we not share your name and address, please check here. ☐

HP08R

*Introducing an exciting debut
from Harlequin Presents!*

Indulge yourself with this intense story
of passion, blackmail and seduction.

VALENTI'S
ONE-MONTH MISTRESS
by Sabrina Philips

Faye fell for the sensual Dante Valenti—but he
took her virginity and left her heartbroken. She
swore *never again!* But he wants her back,
and what Dante wants, Dante takes....

Book #2808

Available March 2009

Look out for more titles from Sabrina Philips
coming soon to Harlequin Presents!

You're invited to join our Tell Harlequin Reader Panel!

By joining our new reader panel you will:

- Receive Harlequin® books—they are FREE and yours to keep with no obligation to purchase anything!
- Participate in fun online surveys
- Exchange opinions and ideas with women just like you
- Have a say in our new book ideas and help us publish the best in women's fiction

In addition, you will have a chance to win great prizes and receive special gifts!
See Web site for details. Some conditions apply.
Space is limited.

To join, visit us at
www.TellHarlequin.com.

Tell
HARLEQUIN